A Heart For Valentine's Day

A Paranormal Erotic Romance

Lexi Esme

Contents

1. Adora 1
2. Adora 10
3. Adora 13
4. Adora 19
5. Aviel 23
6. Adora 35
7. Adora 50
8. Adora 58
9. Aviel 63
10. Aviel 69
11. Adora 80
12. Aviel 90
13. Adora 94
14. Aviel 99
15. Adora 102
16. Adora 116

17. Adora 120
18. Adora 125
19. Adora 135
20. Adora 141
21. Aviel 147
22. Aviel 152
23. Adora 154
24. Aviel 163
25. Aviel 166
26. Adora 176
27. About Author 189
28. THANK YOU FOR READING 191
29. Also By Lexi Esme 192

"I think the new doc wants to hit. No, he's definitely trying to get into my panties."

An Oscar-worthy spit take escapes me, and I just manage to prevent my water from shooting out of my nose.

"You aren't wearing any," I cough, spluttering for breath.

I can hear my sister laughing, and when I look up, she's casually opening a box of tissues from the bedside table. She offers it to me, and I take it, dragging a sheet out and hastily wiping my face. "Damnit, Alecia!"

Alecia's laughter redoubles, but the joyous sound just as quickly disintegrates into a fit of harsh, rattling coughs that rack her whole frame.

My heart aches for her as I watch her struggle for every breath. I shake internally, helplessly watching her body quiver with each violent spasm, desperate to rush to her side and offer comfort. Instead, I wait for the wheezing to subside, using every ounce of willpower I have to stay put. Finally, it becomes too much. I have to force myself to look anywhere but at my sister right now; my heart can't take it. I've been telling myself not to smell this sickly sweet smell or notice how shallow and labored the space between breaths has become, not to see how frail she appears even as she tries to hold herself with pride despite her illness, or allow myself to hear every rattle in her chest as she gathers breath for yet another violent series of coughs that leaves her body quivering.

But she would tear me a new one for fussing, and I don't want this visit to end in an argument. But how can I not show concern, with the doctor's words hammering into my brain? We're running out of time.

My gaze darts around the room from its pale blue walls that fade to white where they meet the ceiling; the television on the far wall is on, set to mute. The window shades are cast open to let in the bright sun; it's surprisingly fair weather for a February day. The outside world simply passes by, oblivious to the life-and-death battle raging in this very room.

What my eyes land on next destroys me.

My sister grasps a few tissues from the box, and I hear her wet and heavy coughs. Recently she's been coughing up blood.

I can't stay still any longer and jolt forward in my seat, desperate to help her, but she halts me withdrawing the tissue from her mouth with a faint grin.

"No blood this time. I'm good," Alecia croaks, revealing a relatively clean tissue.

I breathe a sigh of relief, but I'm still worried.

"You have that big sustainable housing project at work to think about, don't you?" She asks suddenly. "How's that coming along?"

It's obvious what she's trying to do; she's stubborn and hates to see me concerned about her. "It's been coming along well enough, even though they shot down my idea for a community center. I've been working on our team's proposal to send to a few investors; *The Community Renewal Initiative* already sounds interested."

"You need to focus on that," she says, and I open my mouth. "No buts. Work, work, work. You can't fuck this up; you've got your heart set on that promotion anyway." She attempts to sit up straighter in a way that's so characteristic of her and only manages to look pained instead of the regal bearing it's supposed to produce.

Alecia's almond eyes are not what they used to be—they now carry what I know is suppressed pain, and dark circles rest underneath them. Her eyes remain red and puffy from endless nights of sleeping fitfully or not at all. For all her condition has affected her, she is still undeniably beautiful—but at the age of thirty-one, her life was unexpectedly rocked by a diagnosis of cardiomyopathy that left her wasting away.

"I'm more than capable of worrying about work and your health at the same time," I say. Seeing her like this, I can only wish I'd gone into medicine instead.

She winks and fixes me with that broad smile, an expression I could always trust completely. The one I loved, always loved. She's my sister, my rock. I tell myself that she won't leave me like mom and dad did.

Alecia's lips slant up into a lop-sided smile. "The new doc looked at me like I'd make it to Christmas." She utters lightly.

She may as well have been laughing at death itself. "That's not funny," I mutter, my eyes darting away. Still, the tension in the room begins to ease in the aftermath of the episode.

"Better than crying." She shrugs with a hum. "It feels good to laugh. This is what I want to do until I can't do it anymore. If I only have a little while left—why not enjoy it? Just make sure y'all actually choose a cute picture of me for the funeral, or I'm haunting all of y— "

"Stop. It's not your time yet, so don't you dare speak that into existence."

Alecia only rolls her eyes and laughs again.

I never understood why my sister had this never-ending urge to tell such morbid jokes, but perhaps I would do the same if I were in her position. Instead of tears or denial, she chose to laugh—maybe it's the only thing getting us through this unimaginable ordeal.

The doctor's prognosis was that she had two, maybe three weeks if we were lucky. Not years, not months, but weeks. How could I possibly use that sliver of time to save the most important person in my life?

"C'mon, sis," Alecia sighs softly, her deep eyes locking onto mine. "You're serious enough for both of us. It's nice to have someone act normal around me for once."

But nothing is normal about any of this, I want to scream at her. What's normal about being stuck in a hospital bed with a thousand IVs sticking out of her body, a thousand machines beeping their damned alarms because whatever was working just isn't working anymore? Or having her entire life dependent on a waiting list that seems to be getting longer instead of shorter?

"You might be spending Valentine's Day alone this year for real this time," she teases with a sly grin.

My heart feels like it's tripped over itself as those words reach my ears, echoing in the walls of my mind. She has no idea how much that thought terrifies me.

Every year since we were teenagers, we had spent the holiday together because 'Fuck Boys', as my sister so artfully put it. A decade later, and here we are still carrying on the tradition, all because Alecia's old flame from years ago had stood her up for a Valentine's Day date. Very mature of us, of course. But now I really can be alone this year because, in a few weeks' time, my sister could be dead.

With a tight smile, I try to shove down my emotions, "I can't believe you." Despite myself, my eyes sting with tears, "What happened to fuck boys?"

Alecia chortles weakly, her lips tugging into a smirk. "But Dr. Hanson isn't a boy. I saw his dick print; that's a man--"

"Please don't," I beg. "I'd like to talk to the man with a straight face the next time I see him." A burst of laughter escapes between us both.

"Maybe you could fuck him, it's cuffing season anyway, and you look like you need it." I glare at my sister as she laughs and flips me the middle finger. "You need to put a ring on that finger sooner or later."

"That is not where the ring goes."

Alecia continues laughing. But I can sense what she's implying beneath all that laughter and the jokes; her need for me not to be alone when she's gone. Her desire for me to have some strength and courage of my own. Suddenly, her courage becomes all too real to me. She's already accepted what's waiting for her at the end of the battle that she's fighting with everything in her.

"Whatever, the important thing right now is that you do everything possible to deliver an amazing presentation. You can take a couple of days off to be with me, but no matter what, promise me you'll keep going." Alecia lifts herself up on her hands, suppressing a cough. "Well, I won't keep you, but know that I'm proud of you."

"Stop making everything sound so final." I try to smile back, "You'll have plenty of time to be proud of me."

But there isn't time for more small talk. The coughing soon returns with a vengeance, and blood now coats her lips and runs down her chin. I rush to the call button, desperate for the nurse to get here fast and help, just as Alecia's hand clutches her chest.

The nurse ushers me out of the room and into the hall as she administers oxygen, and Alecia's grip on her chest tightens. All I can hear is the dull hum of fluorescent lights, the hissing of the oxygen machine, and the heart monitor beeps.

Time stands still while I wait outside, agonizing over whether this will be Alecia's last day alive. It feels like hours before I can see the doctor, and when I finally do, my chest constricts, and I find myself fighting back the urge to cry again.

I enter Dr. Hanson's small medical office and sit with trepidation opposite him at his desk.

"Miss Coleman," he says in greeting with a gentle smile and sympathetic eyes. His calm grey eyes radiate a warm and reassuring aura, combined with his stature and handsomely coiffed sandy hair with a distinguished wave, it's easy to understand why my sister is so taken with him.

I hate that I can't hate this man for his inability to save my sister, even though I know it isn't his fault.

"Dr. Hanson," I reply, then murmur, "I'm sorry we couldn't talk more yesterday."

He graciously shakes his head. "Not at all; I understand. Everyone's grieving process is different, and you've been going through a difficult time." There's genuine sorrow in his voice.

Yesterday, he told me there was no hope for my sister without surgery, and unfortunately, no heart was available for the transplant. But I couldn't handle it, so I broke down and cried. He had no choice but to wait until I composed myself. I don't know how long it took me to calm down.

"I'm sorry—I thought she was having a good day today," I say with a quivering voice, trying to move the focus away from me. I struggle to push back another torrent of tears and desperately seek some glimmer of hope that perhaps things could be different this time.

Dr. Hanson smiles faintly, "Your sister really is a force of nature, Ms. Coleman," he pauses before continuing with a solemn tone, "But nothing has changed regarding her condition, I'm sorry to say."

I feel my shoulders sag.

He clears his throat before continuing, "You might want to look into hospice care to ensure her comfort in her final days—"

I cut him off with an indignant shout. "No!" My voice echoes in the chamber, startling us both. I steady my breath and declare more calmly, slowly, "No sir, I won't give up on my sister. Taking her home just to wait for her to die? That's not an option I'm willing to accept, no matter what fancy term you call it."

Dr. Hanson remains silent, possibly assessing my sanity, but I don't care. How can I make him understand that while Alecia was just another patient to him, to me, she was all I had? She had been a parent to me when we'd lost our mom and dad; she'd been my sister when I needed support and my best friend when I needed someone to call.

Alecia went to night school and simultaneously worked a job to put food on the table for the both of us. And when she found her passion was caring for others, she even gave back to the community, volunteering whenever she could—until she suddenly couldn't, because that's just how Alecia was.

How did I make the doctor understand that I couldn't give up? If the roles were reversed, Alecia wouldn't hesitate to steal a heart if it meant saving me.

The thought makes me pause as everything suddenly falls into place: Alecia *would* steal a heart if she had to! A shiver runs through me, and that's all the resolve I need.

"Ms. Coleman?" Dr. Hanson's voice pulls me back to the present, his brow creased with confusion. Had he been calling my name?

I snap my head up, guilt already coursing through my veins as his face comes into focus.

"I'm sorry, doctor," I say, unable to keep the fear from my voice. "What were you saying?"

"Your sister was the one to suggest we start looking into palliative care," he says after a moment.

This realization makes me tear up, but my resolve deepens. Alecia may be unable to fight anymore, but I can do it in her stead. "I'll get started on making arrangements right away."

I rise quickly from the chair and don't even hear the last words he says to me as I grab the brochures he offers me from his desk and stuff them in my bag before turning towards the door. Before I even reach it, his last words are already lost in my wake.

Alecia has been on the heart transplant wait list for well over six months now, but she doesn't have any more months left in her. The hospital staff has done all they can, and now it's my turn to step up and take matters into my own hands, regardless of the repercussions.

I'd done the same when we initially got Alecia's diagnosis, and the healthcare system had failed us miserably anyway.

Initially, every doctor we visited had been dismissive of Alecia's complaints of fatigue, palpitations, and breathlessness. One had gotten visibly impatient; another hastily diagnosed her with anxiety and suggested she needed to relax more. Others attested that her numbers looked okay and couldn't imagine what could be wrong. After ruling out all the usual suspects, they sent us on our way without answers. But I knew better; I just knew that something was wrong, and unfortunately, the medical system didn't always take the concerns of women, and women of color at that, seriously.

I spent night after night searching for solutions, pouring over medical journals and articles, grasping at any hint or clues I could find. In the end, it took several doctors and multiple opinions to find one that took her suffering seriously. Finally, we found a doctor who would listen to us with compassion, Dr. Morgan - an angel disguised in a doctor's coat - who vowed to get to the bottom of the medical mystery and began running extensive tests. Only then could we put a name to the culprit; myocardiopathy, caused by a genetic defect of the heart. But the diagnosis came too late; her heart was beyond repair. All the time we were in the dark left us little time to treat her, leaving me with an impossible task - to find my sister a heart.

I return to the table, this time with sustenance for us all: mugs of steamy hot cocoa for all to fight back winter's seasonal chill. Helen, my good friend and next-door neighbor, lifts her head of brown and blonde streaked ringlets, glancing up from the monitor over her boyfriend's shoulder.

Both inhale deeply as I place the mugs on the table, the sweet aroma of rich chocolate, cinnamon, and nutmeg wafting through the air. We all pick up our cocoa and sip slowly, savoring every drop.

Before long, Helen throws me a guarded glance, "Adora, you *absolutely* sure about this?" She asks me for the fifth time, her sharp eyebrows knitting together tightly with worry.

My fingers tremble as I firmly grip the warm mug in my hands. The cryptic and vague DMs hold my gaze transfixed on the screen, yet my answer remains the same. No, I am *not* sure about meeting some man I'd met on the dark web, but yes, I am definitely going because, despite how effed up it is, I have no other choice.

Helen's boyfriend, Tayo, was the genius who had done the internet research and helped me set up a meeting three days ago with the username SacredHeart. The location and fine details are being established and finalized today.

"Okay, here it is." Tayo's lanky frame swings around in his seat, his elbow draped over the chair backing as he hands me a single sheet of notebook paper with the address written across it in a haphazard scrawl, "It's all there. Check-in is at 8pm."

I look at it, nod once, and clutch the paper tightly, feeling the weight of expectation in the air.

After work, I was to go downtown to the place SacredHeart specified, if it was even a 'he.' There is no photo or phone number, just a meeting place; the backstreet between Rosewood Avenue and Nightingale Street is near the I.E.D. Pub. That's all I have, that and the desperate hope that this meeting will lead to the vital organ I so urgently sought.

Helen gives Tayo a rough nudge, and he jerks forward.

"Ow!" Tayo yelps, cradling his shoulder, "Girl, what'd you do that for?"

"We're *both* going with you, obviously," Helen declares, her voice laced with no-nonsense determination. Her seafoam eyes narrow expectantly at him. "Right?"

Tayo grabs his smartwatch and knits his brows together at the screen, "But I'm on a deadline, and I still have to develop--"

Helen thumps him hard on the shoulder, "You were saying?"

Tayo heaves a deep sigh and rolls his eyes, resigned to his fate. "Fine. Forget the app for the start-up; we're going with you, Adora."

She adds, turning to look at me this time, "You won't be alone—and don't give me any arguments about it. We wanna see this guy too and make sure he's not some creep trying to snatch you up."

My heart flutters with anxiety at the thought of burdening them, desperation however, outweighs my modesty. I smile gratefully and nod in agreement. "I mean, he's got connects to an organ trafficking ring...I'm pretty sure that it's impossible for him not to be a creep. But, thanks a lot guys, I swear, I'll make it up to you both somehow—"

Tayo shakes his head, and reassures me with a gentle smile, "You're our girl, don't worry about it. We'll be right behind you." He reaches over and gives Helen's hand a tender squeeze. Helen returns the gesture, and smiles at him, then presses a kiss to the stubble of his dark cheek.

I watch their love with a mixture of admiration and nostalgia—reminding me that even amidst the ills in this world there really is still hope for a brighter future, and right now, that hope lies with Sacred-Heart.

This is undeniably the most dangerous and moronic thing that I will ever do. My mind rolls over the possible outcomes; either I will save my sister's life or end up lying at the bottom of some murky river.

"I won't take my eyes off her, I swear," Tayo says, adjusting his glasses.

"You better not," Helen says.

Tayo may look fragile with his long frame and mild face, but he was the only one who could find this guy in the first place. I couldn't help but be thankful for his presence and loyalty.

Helen would stay home due to a minor cold; her pecan skin and cherry-red nose a painful contrast. I had to beg her to, concerned that her health would only worsen if she came with us.

I watch as Helen gives Tayo a goodbye peck before wishing both of us luck, and then we head out.

Tayo and I are silent the entire way there. I can feel his worry radiating from him, heightening my own anxieties. My stomach churns with each passing mile. Arriving now, the destination lies just ahead, and I feel like throwing up when the car finally slows to a stop. Tayo parks in a strategic place where he can see me, and I move to open the car door and meet the guy alone as instructed.

Tayo puts a gentle hand on my shoulder before I leave. "Adora, if you notice anything shady about him—anything at all, get out of there as fast as you can and meet me at the car. Okay?" He waits until I nod my agreement before finally allowing me to slip out of the passenger seat.

I get out and walk to the corner of the backstreet as instructed. There, like a beacon in the night, is the teddy bear used as a marker, and I know that somewhere nearby, SacredHeart is waiting. But no sound breaks the air, no movement disturbs the shadows. I wait and pray for a miracle, but all that greets me is dead silence and unending minutes. Checking my phone for the umpteenth time, I realize that forty minutes have passed since my arrival.

He really isn't coming. Despondent, I bend to place the teddy bear on the ground. I should have known, it was too good to be true. Turning away, I prepare to head back, my hopes smashed like fragile glass on a stone floor.

“Leaving so soon?” The deep baritone sends a chill down my spine.

I whirl around, my breath catching in my throat as from the shadows emerges a terrifying figure. His dark clothing hangs from his massive frame, numerous piercings adorn his face, he wears his hair in a pale shorn buzz-cut, and the broad smile he gives me shows off yellowed teeth.

“Why don’t we take a little walk, I’m sure your boyfriend won’t mind,” he says.

Knowing that he’s been watching me for so long is almost as bad as the suggestion that I leave my only lifeline, Tayo, behind. But something in my gut tells me that there is absolutely no way this guy is going to give me what I want if I don’t do as he says. So, shoving every

Criminal Minds episode I've ever watched to the back of my mind, I follow SacredHeart.

The building grounds we walk into have every filthy scenario imaginable, and it shocks me that barely an hour away from my home is this devastatingly wretched place.

Its exterior is grimy and barely maintained, the dilapidated outer walls covered in the crudest graffiti. The bars on the front-facing windows are rusted. The only thing pristine about it is the fresh dusting of snow on the sills from earlier this evening.

The stench of alcohol clings to the air as I step over used needles and strewn garbage littering the ground.

This is the underbelly of our society, where anything goes, and I wonder if I am any different now that I have chosen to do this. Adora –once a first-class environmental science graduate– would have died first before coming to this place. But now I wonder how much that Adora has changed; I am no longer her. Now, I am just Adora, the woman who is about to lose her sister.

"So, how long?" he asks as I trudge alongside him.

"How long?" I echo in confusion, and he lets out a heavy sigh, as he punches a code into the keypad, then pulls open the door to the entrance. He walks right in, and I have to sprint to slip inside behind him.

As soon as I cross the threshold, I blink. Compared to the streets outside, the inside of the apartment is a shock; the walls are painted egg-shell white, the floor lined with glossy black marbled tiling, and overlaid with a thick runner carpet. It's warm with central heating, a relief from the chill of the streets outside.

"How long before the ticker stops?" He asks again, his voice impatient and sharp.

"She has advanced cardiomyopathy, and it's-"

"Enough of your medical jargon," he cuts me off, "I don't care if she's been shot in the chest, I need to know your time frame. You said it's urgent. How urgent is it?"

"Two weeks, maybe less," I reply, swallowing the ball of emotion building up in my throat.

"Hm," is all he responds.

I glance around; this isn't the apartment of someone who is down and out. Nor does the seemingly infinite amount of monitors lining the living room wall and the bank of monitors atop the desk make sense for someone destitute. A woman wearing glasses sits behind the desk typing away intensely at her keyboard.

"My girl Nancy here," he says, gesturing to the lady who reminds me so much of Tayo, save for in phenotype, "She's been looking, and the best I can do is a month or so."

I clutch my chest in panic, feeling my heart pound and blood surge through my veins. "Please, we don't have that much time!"

"This isn't a liver we are talking about here, sweet cheeks. Unless you're offering yours, then I can't make that shit happen in a couple of days," He says with a casual shrug of the shoulders.

That thought had already crossed my mind once or twice, but no science magic could be done about my sister and I's incompatible blood groups.

A wave of nausea threatens to overtake me again, and I turn away from the man to try to calm myself.

"We can get you up the list if you can pay."

I round on him, "I am just coming from a list, and you are telling me that I have to be on another one?!" I can't believe this! The whole point of these guys was that they didn't have lists!

"Nine hundred thousand, and you'll have it tomorrow," he replies without hesitation.

I almost laugh in his face; did I look like I had that kind of money? I'm still mired in student debt, and my entry-level salary is nothing to write home about. My company was already helping out with a loan, but it is only a measly twenty thousand. Factoring in what I can sell and what I can borrow, I still would never get to that amount in a couple of weeks.

I stumble aimlessly towards the nearest chair, slump into the seat and bury my face in my hands. This is it. I am going to lose my sister and there's nothing I can do to stop the inevitable.

SacredHeart tried to offer some payment options but they were all still impossible, and I find myself trudging back through a swirling snowdrift to Tayo's car empty-handed some twenty minutes later. I can't stop the tears, and I have to stop for a moment to get myself together before I can face Tayo with the awful news.

The crunching of snow under swift footfalls makes me look back, only to find Nancy behind me, her coat rippling in the cold wind. She strides closer, her eyes stern and determined as she grips my hand, pressing a small paper into it and not letting go.

"Listen, he can help you. But be careful, he's..." she says in a near-whisper, but her voice trails off with a fear that I have never heard before and my heart throbs in response. Whatever it is, it clearly isn't good.

"They say he isn't human; ruthless, some might say," she finally says, "But word is he can get anything. If you have no other options, you need him."

I peer into her pale blue eyes, words failing me, but the question clear in my gaze. Why is she trying to help me?

"I've been there too," is her soft reply before she squeezes my hand. "Just—just be careful, okay? When he gives something, he always wants something back in return."

I'm lost in thought for a moment, but just as soon, the reason I started this journey comes back to me. Alecia's life is on the line, this is my only chance, and I'm going to save her no matter what.

I give a resolute nod and walk back to Tayo with a renewed sense of hope in my heart. I don’t care about being careful anymore, I only care about Alecia, and the piece of paper in my grasp is my ticket to finding her a heart.

Helen grips my shoulders firmly and pulls me into the living room of her and Tayo's apartment. Her unwavering gaze holds more weight than her hands do.

"You have to tell me what happened," she says, her voice tight with urgency. "Everything."

I finish telling my story and the room falls into a dense silence. I've never seen Helen so still.

"That woman only gave you a damn phone number?" she asks, her voice laced with both disbelief and fear.

"Yeah," I reply, staring at the nine digits in my hand, my stomach coiled tightly.

“Do you at least have a name for who you'll be meeting?” Helen probes further.

“Someone who can help,” I shrug, folding the number back up and trying to sound confident, but my nerves are getting the best of me.

“So no name, then,” Tayo concludes quietly as he returns from retrieving the food delivery. He sets a paper bag of Jamaican take-out on the table and starts to unpack it.

I shake my head and take a deep breath.

He frowns. “You can't seriously be thinking about going to see this guy," he says, proceeding to lift out a container of pepperpot soup for Helen, who utters a ‘thank you, babe,’ in return, and then Styrofoam clamshell containers filled with jerk chicken, fried plantains, coleslaw and rice and peas for us.

“Thanks.” I push down my fear and meet Tayo's gaze as I reply firmly: “I’m not thinking about it. I’m going to do it."

"A burner phone number, an undisclosed address, no name,” Helen ticks off each point with her fingers. She pauses to look me in the eye and swears, “Do you realize what this could mean? You could end up in a trafficking situation for all we know!”

“This has been a trafficking situation, remember?” I try to joke as I chew on a fried plantain slice.

But the mood only sobers further as they exchange worried looks.

I clear my throat and, seeking courage, gulp from my bottle of Red Stripe. My sister's morbid humor doesn't work for me as well as it does for her. At least the alcohol is helping me calm down.

I have to remain strong for the sake of my sister, despite the odds, and our dwindling finances, even if the thought of meeting someone about whom rumors of inhumanity run rampant sends a wave of unease through me. I keep this fact to myself, Tayo and Helen's reactions to that little tidbit would only exacerbate my own doubts.

I declare confidently, "Hey, I won't get trafficked. I don't have many other choices, and I can't accept any more money from you two. You’re both saving up for a down payment on a house - I won't let you dip into it to spot me for medical expenses again."

"Adora-" Helen protests.

“It really isn’t an issue, Alecia is like family to us too.” Tayo adds.

I shake my head, "I'm gonna do this."

"But at what cost?" Helen asks in frustration, her voice wavering slightly. "You don't even know who you're dealing with."

"I know, but I have to trust my gut, and I believe this guy--whoever he is--can get Alecia what she needs," I reply, trying to keep the conversation light. "Besides, you'll be the first to know if something goes wrong. You'll be able to track me down with this burner phone number and come to my rescue."

"Ha! You're so funny," Helen scoffs, rolling her eyes. "I'm serious, Adora. You need to be careful."

"I know, I know," I say, holding up my hands in surrender.

Tayo puts his beer down, his gaze hard, "We can't let you go alone. We'll follow behind you in my car in case something goes wrong. Just give us the address and we'll wear disguises if necessary."

The notion of them dressing up in disguises makes a smile quirk my lips. "Uh-uh, not happening," I say. "I told you, it's part of the deal. They specifically said no plus ones allowed. It's too risky; they'll see you and the car will drive off along with my last chance." I release a heavy sigh. "I've already set up an appointment. They're going to have someone pick me up tomorrow, and we'll see if we can work out a deal. Apparently, this guy, whoever he is, is really anal about who he works with."

"This whole thing still sounds sketchy as hell to me," Helen rubs her forehead, irritation clear on every feature.

I merely shrug.

Tayo and Helen exchange another tense glance, their concern for my well-being clear. I have to look away.

"I don't like this, Adora," Helen finally says.

Tayo shifts uneasily in his chair. I can see his frustration and realize how deeply we all feel the burden of my decision.

"Well do you have a better option?" My voice shakes as I speak, "Either of you?"

Silence hangs heavy in the air as Tayo and Helen both lower their heads, a sense of defeat settling over us all. I know they've done everything in their power to help me, but at this point, there's nothing else any of us can do.

I can't help but think about the twists and turns that life can take. One moment, you can feel like your dreams are finally coming to fruition, and the next, you're grasping at straws, desperate for a lifeline. But, in those moments, that's where you find the strength and courage to do what needs to be done.

I take a deep breath, my determination solidifying within me. "I really appreciate you two."

Helen closes her eyes, and her shoulders slump in resignation, bracing for the worst. Tayo sits there with his mouth twisted into a grim expression. He yanks his beer off the table again and takes a deep swig before finally making one last plea. "Just promise us," he says sternly, locking eyes with me. "Promise us you'll be careful."

"I will," I nod.

"I believe you should go on a diet, Lilith; you are getting rather fat."

Lilith lets out a menacing hiss as she slithers towards me, her eyes intently fixed on the dripping heart in my palm; her tongue flickers out as she creeps closer to inspect the treat.

"But I believe this one was vegan, so it should be safe," I remark with a chuckle, skimming my fingers along the smooth glistening scales of her back. Her fanged maw gapes wide, and she engulfs the heart whole. "Good girl..."

A stifled gasp echoes in my office, and my eyes stray to the corner where my still-living debtor, Mosley, stands in the shadows. He's sweating profusely, his wide watery eyes darting between me and the corpse on the floor. Fear twists his features, changing his pallid complexion to a sickly hue—and the air is thick with the smell of it. He's still waiting anxiously, albeit quietly as he was told, to be addressed.

His reaction is a bit of an exaggeration, in my opinion. The corpse before him was someone who dared to try to steal from me after I had so graciously helped him turn his small construction company into a multinational development conglomerate. And how does he repay me after a decade-long partnership? By betraying the first person to have ever had faith in him, of course, and attempting to avoid paying up on the debt he accrued. In addition to just plain managing the corporation sloppily. It's to be expected, though, such is the nature of his kind.

Now he lays on the floor in a puddle of his own blood, his chest opened and hollowed of its once beating heart. Hopefully, his successor will serve more capably and honestly than he ever did. If they're smart, they'll see this as a golden opportunity to obtain my favor. For now, the old head of Keystone Builders had made his bed, and now he was lying in it; rather, I made certain he died in it.

"I'm sorry you had to see that," I say, "I'm afraid my careless assistant double-booked my appointments for the day. But, I want to assure you, you'll be taken care of as well. Just give me a moment while I get this cleaned up."

I observe my assistant's silent labor. Jerry? Or is it James? No matter, my aide wheels the body away along with my bloodied robe. Such a shame, I liked that dressing gown. At the very least, it allowed me to give my tattoos some fresh air.

Jay slips out to dispose of the corpse, and I'm left alone in the still, silent air that smells heavily of death, and fear. I've long been accustomed to these particular scents.

My thoughts are broken when Mosley decides to make his next mistake—he speaks up out of turn, interrupting my contemplation and drawing my attention. I doubt Mosley's next comment is made out of malice; he's just too stupid to realize what he says:

"I just need one more day—please!" He throws himself to his knees on the ground in a disgusting display, his sweaty palms clasped together. "I was going to pay them back!"

I step around him to finish the dead thief's paperwork, with a single click of my pen, signing off and closing the file permanently. I hate unfinished business.

"I wasn't trying to run!" He gasps just as Lilith hisses at him with a lunge, sending him further into a frenzy, and a fresh burst of fear rises into the air anew as he scrambles back.

"Down, Lilith. That's not very nice." But my gaze is cold as I slowly turn my attention to him, my voice dripping with poison. I take a step closer, looming over his shrinking form. "Well, Mosley, what were you trying to do?" I wonder aloud. "Why did you go no contact? Why did my assistant have to find you halfway across the state?"

Mosley attempts an answer, but only gibberish escapes his lips. His fear is palpable, so thick in the air you can breathe it in.

"You *weren't* trying to shirk your payment for services rendered?" I narrow my eyes peering down at him.

"I had someone I was meeting up with this morning, I was getting the money to pay the lender back!"

I shake my head, the man always did work on his own terms. My lips curl into a spiteful smirk. "You were supposed to have the money last night at midnight. What do you suggest I tell the lenders now?"

He shakes his head frantically, trying to mumble out an explanation.

My patience has worn thin, and I interrupt him with a snarl. "Enough." I stride forward, my hand seizing upon the bloody carving knife still on the ground. "We will settle this." I raise it up to the light, watching as it glints and reflects off its sharp, red-stained edge. I offer it to him by the blade with a daring glare, willing him to take it.

Mosley shakes his head desperately, staring at it, not daring to move an inch closer to me or the knife. I can sense his hesitation and act on it quickly, latching onto his hand and forcing it onto the blade.

Tilting my head slightly, I say, "There might be other payment options...so how about I offer you an alternative? You can choose to pay me what you owe in blood."

The man holds the knife, his hand trembling. I am, of course, unyielding but fair. "Two-thirds of your liver, a single kidney, your spleen, or either hand. Choose one."

The man holds the knife, turning it over in his hand. I'm sure he is weighing his options, wondering what piece of himself he can afford to lose. I've been fair with Mosley and expect no less from him in return.

Mosley looks at me with wide horrified eyes as if he is seeing me as something alien and terrible—a little boy who had just seen a wolf lurking in the shadow of a tree for the very first time. His face crumples up, and he begins to sob.

His fear and anguish are intoxicating, I move closer as if to console him, but I offer no warmth or sympathy. "And make sure you choose wisely. As soon as you are decided, we can begin the extraction."

"Don't do this," he begs desperately between fat tears. "Please don't."

"I haven't done anything, Mosley. This is your doing," I admonish him sternly, my voice still soft.

His hands begin to shake violently, and he buries his face in them, shuddering violently with sobs that shake his frame from head to toe.

"Take your time," I purr into the silence between us, watching him intently as he trembles on the brink of despair — weighing his options. As if they matter now, I already know what he'll do. I knew it from the start of our association. I watch as all hope slips away from him like the last few grains of sand through an hourglass. I know what will come next, and this moment is only an illusion of choice.

"I'll give you a moment." I rise to my feet and turn away from him to examine my wristwatch, feigning disinterest in his misery.

But I can hear him rise to his feet behind me, his breaths quickening, harshening. I whirl around in time to see his eyes bulge in anticipation, locking with mine as he lunges forward. Just as his knife reaches me I snatch his wrist and squeeze, and the knife drops from his fingers with a clatter. A desperate cry pierces the air as he realizes his defeat.

I'm on him before he can move, my fingers digging into the tender flesh of his neck. His feet thrash fruitlessly as I lift him from the ground, choking off the last remnants of hope from a soul that no longer comprehends its fate.

"Exactly as I thought." I sneer coldly, and in anticipation of the next moment, the tattoos along my flesh writhe in a frenzy. Mosley's eyes bulge further, if possible, and his gurgling is all that comes back to me. "You think I couldn't see what you truly were all along?—Just another terrified, cowardly rat who would turn on the only man who helped him as soon as his back is turned."

I hold him firmly in place as Lilith winds her way around my leg, prepared to feast on the morsel of flesh he will provide.

Alas, her meal is not meant to be. "This one is not for you, Lilith."

With a flick of my wrist, Mosley hurtles through the air and hits the far end of the room, the impact knocking framed paintings from their stations on the wall, and he slides into a slouch among them.

Winded, he wheezes heavily, fetching for breath, his hands grasping at his bruised throat.

"Fortunately for you, Mosley, the debt is already paid. I promised the lender that my client would keep his word, and I always keep mine."

Mosley's head snaps up, and he blinks his bleary eyes, not comprehending. "You mean you— ? You...you paid my debt?" He scuttles toward me on his hands and knees in reverence, planting kisses atop my polished shoes. “Thank you, Aviel!—I'm sorry!— I will never forget your kindness! Thank you!”

I only echo him: “Thank...you?”

He peers up slowly.

"I bought your debt. But my interest rate is far more exorbitant than what your creditors sought.” His eyes widen in horror. He scrambles back from me once again.

"W-what do you mean?" He stammers but now with a newfound fear.

"You have nothing to worry about," I smile coldly, and as I say it, his tears pause. "Your debt is absolved, all I need is your soul." And before he has time to even comprehend what is happening to him, Mosley’s body begins to crumble into a pile of ash at my feet.

As for me, I had acquired another tattoo on my arm: A petrified black rat forever etched into my skin as a reminder of this day and the debt I exacted from him.

My assistant trails in through the door, and I utter in a clipped tone: “When you return with the next appointment, bring them to my study, it smells like blood and death in here.”

He gives a single bow of his head and leaves the room, and I use the time to take a relaxing shower and wash the blood away. Then prepare for my next meeting.

Funny creatures, humans are. So full of their own hubris, they felt so powerful and invincible, yet when tested by truth, they recognize just how fearful, fragile, and fleeting they really are. Take Lilith’s dessert, for example, he’d been a wealthy, powerful man, but it had only taken a single bullet to reduce that grand legacy to nothing. And that’s exactly what anyone will find of him when his body is fully processed. His sudden disappearance never to be solved. Terrible for him indeed, but oh so wonderful for business.

Speaking of business, a wonderful scent permeates my house as soon as my two o'clock appointment steps in. There is nothing quite like desperation to fuel my reason for being on earth, and this one smells utterly delicious. Her heart would make for fine dining for Lilith once I was done with her. As if reading my thoughts, Lilith weaves between my legs and winds herself around my calf.

I draw in the sweet aroma with a thick sniff, a fine wine in my senses, as Lilith continues to climb up, "You smell it too, don't you?"

Her hiss echoes through the air, as she slowly crawls up until she reaches my back, and I bid her stay put atop my shoulders. Her well-fed body is a weight I have grown accustomed to; she settles in her favorite place and falls asleep, sinking deep into my flesh.

I scent my assistant guiding my visitor through the foyer. Their smells are so different, yet still so intoxicating. One filled with so much resentment and the other with such pure unadulterated desperation, it almost makes me lick my lips. I take in another deep breath before exiting the bathroom and making my way to the study, where my unsuspecting guest awaits.

I push open the solid mahogany wood doors of the meeting room, and her eyes catch mine the moment I cross the threshold. They are nothing like what I am so used to seeing. Deep, with a hint of softness and vulnerability, both intriguing and captivating, but also filled with sadness, as if they carry within them the weight of the world. Those brown eyes are framed by dark lashes that brush lightly against her cheeks, fluttering with each blink, making her all the more hypnotizing.

The petite woman stands motionless among the shadows in the center of the room. Her nutmeg skin is a perfect canvas for her trim curves, a narrow waist that trails to hips fit for the hands of a man. Her hair is neat, cropped close to the scalp, and the features it frames are both soft, and delicate. Such an innocent thing is something I didn't see much around here. Which makes me wonder how she has come to be here at all.

For a fleeting moment, I allow myself to be transfixed by this rare vision before me.

My guest's eyes begin to trace the corners of the room feverishly — from the vaulted ceilings to the heavy velvet curtains draped across the walls, and long shelves lined with books. As she turns her head to gaze about, I see her soft hair has a subtle texture that catches the light ever so delicately.

I let the door shut behind me and inwardly smile at the quickening of her breath as she realizes that no one else will be joining us. Finally, she stands stark still on the thick Oriental rug.

"Sir, this is Adora Coleman." Jude finally breaks the silence and my trance.

I wave my assistant away with a dismissing flick of my wrist, yet my fascination with the woman before me prevents me from averting my gaze, her growing uncertainty only intensifying my intrigue and filling me with anticipation. I gesture to the nearby armchair, indicating for her to take a seat, and she does while I take the seat opposite her.

"What brings you to me?" I inquire, maintaining a smooth and inviting tone, my eyes drinking in the desperation on her face.

She looks me up and down nervously before her gaze finally settles on mine. Her lips quiver as she searches for the words to explain her plight. As she starts to tell me of the nature of her visit, I can't help but linger on the full lips coated in a glistening balm, as they move softly while recounting an unenviable tale of hardship, disappointment, and dashed hopes before she finishes with an earnest plea: "My sister is dying, and I really need your help."

I can't help but smirk in amusement and lean closer to her, "I don't know what you've heard about me, but I think you have the wrong idea. 'Helping' isn't exactly my specialty."

Adora's voice trembles, but now her stare is unwavering and captivating, "What about getting a heart? Is that something you can do?"

Well that, I hadn't been expecting.

I relax back into my own chair and let my eyes slow-roam her, settling on her quivering hands. The manicured nails gnawed away, raw and vulnerable. Beautiful. Nothing like the vile humans I came across every day, but she is still in my house all the same. Which makes her fair game. To me, she is an enticing opportunity presented on a silver platter. This damsel in distress would find no solace here.

"It can be done," I say non-commitally, feigning fascination with my own fingernails and willing myself to stay impassive despite the thrill that surges through me when she very nearly leaps from her chair.

"Really?"

"I could make a call or two. Depends on what's in it for me?" My gaze darts back to hers, and I relish the way she flinches.

Adora clears her throat and manages to dial back her enthusiasm before asking, "How much do you charge? And can it all be done within the week?"

Despite her best efforts, I can still hear the underlying eagerness behind her words, the unruly pounding of her heart.

I wonder idly if her sister truly is worth all of this effort—likely not. But business is business. There was something about Adora that I wanted - and there was no way I could let this one go without taking something back in return.

The atmosphere thickens, and I welcome the heavy quiet that fills the room.

"How about two days?" I say and watch her entire face light up with relief, while misguided hope blooms in her eyes.

A silly, desperate human. Too naïve for her own good.

"You can do that?" She breathes.

"I know some people who can," I reply with a measured tone.

"Please," she says, resolute. "I'll do whatever it takes to save her."

That is music to my ears. It's always such a joy exposing and exploiting the weaknesses of humans—that weakness usually being their fear.

"When money is involved, miracles can happen," I reply with finality and rise to retrieve a contract from my desk drawer, and begin drawing it up. "You'll need an expert surgeon to put that heart in your sister's chest and money to pay that surgeon. I know some talented individuals who will make sure your case gets utmost priority."

"Thank-you," she says with a quiver in her voice, and it's almost enough to give me pause.

"I'm merely doing my job, Adora." I shrug, trying to ignore her expression of gratitude. "There is a matter of the paperwork—tedious, I know, but it must be done." I slide the papers across the solid wood desk to her, "Two hundred thousand, payable in two weeks to the day—don't forget that." I pick up my signing pen and turn back towards her, despite my efforts, I can't quite stop my lips from curving into an anticipatory leer as I continue speaking. "If you fail to pay on time for any reason, it will accrue fifty percent interest daily."

She nods, and I grant her the utensil. I watch her carefully as she fills in the blanks. The paper crackles as she runs her pen across it, her breathing rapid and shallow. Her concentration is intense as she makes sure to dot every "i" and cross every "t" before she returns the signed copy to me.

I flash a smile at her, and she looks slightly tense but attempts a small smile in return.

"Ah, you forgot the back," I say archly, wrinkling my nose with a sneer and pushing the papers back to her.

A curse, soft but audible, escapes her lips before she hastily signs it too.

The fool.

"Done." She says sharply and thrusts the contract back to me with a defiant look, and I take my time with it, if only to prolong this moment. Her gaze nearly burns holes through the sheet while she frustrates, awaiting my own signature.

"You are taking a huge risk here, considering the operation might not go the way you want it to." I point out patronizingly and with a mild air of warning.

She narrows her eyes and clenches her fists as if she's holding back from telling me off. Too bad, I would love to see that.

"I know, but my sister is a fighter," Adora replies stiffly, her hand trembling as she clutches her purse.

Our eyes meet for a few moments, and I finally speak in a slow and even voice, "Fight it as you may, no one truly conquers death, Adora."

"I'm determined to try," she says, her voice soft yet strong.

My mouth almost twitches into a smile, but I push the feeling away. I nod and decide to let her have this round, "My assistant will show you out and have everything arranged for your sister." With that said and done, my signature finally makes its way onto the paper.

She springs to her feet and wipes her palms against her pants. The weight she had come in carrying has been lifted, and I can sense the subtle change in her, her aura is full of relief now. The seed of uncertainty that I had tried to plant hadn't taken root, she was not going to give up on her sister. Funny thing, that human sibling obligation. I'll never have an appreciation for it since it seems more of a burden than anything else. But my guest is leaving for now, and I'll have more time to dissect her in the coming days.

"Thank you again, Mister -?"

"Aviel." I say, my gaze perhaps lingering a moment too long as I speak my name. "Please, call me Aviel."

For the hundredth time, my eyes wander around the waiting room, meandering from the sparse furniture, the walls painted in a ghostly grey, a faint backdrop to the small piles of out-of-date magazines strewn about.

Through the single frosted window, I can make out a bleak grey sky, ashen against the stark white of the limestone buildings, decorated by half-frozen vines, their tendrils dappled with a light dusting of snow.

Alecia's been in surgery for a few hours now, and my anxiety grows with each passing minute.

With a sigh, I attempt, once again, to pour over the funding applications in front of me. I brought my project portfolio along with me, thinking I might be able to get some headway on the project, but my mind is having none of it. All I manage to accomplish is re-read the forms I'll be sending to *Housing for Humanity, Green Builders,* and *The Community Renewal Initiative.*

As I struggle to concentrate on the task in front of me, I sense a presence looming from above, and the hairs on my neck prickle with anticipation. Before I have the chance to look up, a voice descends on me in a velvet timbre, reverberating with an icy undercurrent that sends shivers down my spine: "I thought you could use this."

I cautiously glance up and find the figure of Aviel standing over me in the makeshift waiting room, peering down at me with narrowed black eyes — so dark they seem to swallow all the light around them.

Apparently, he'd brought a styrofoam cup of steaming coffee with him, its robust aroma subduing the clinical smell of the room, bringing a flicker of comfort. My stomach rumbles hungrily, but the thought of eating or drinking anything right now does nothing for my appetite. I have to admit, the company is a welcome distraction as I wait anxiously for news about my sister.

"Thank you," I murmur hastily, making him smile, my eyes only briefly stray to the length and sharpness of his canine teeth before quickly averting away. There is something about that smile that is part alluring, and part warning, evoking incomprehensible feelings within me, like something lurks quiet beneath the veil of his tranquil facade.

Aviel is tall and dark-haired with striking features; piercing, near-black eyes, and sharp cheekbones. He's broad-shouldered, his body chiseled with lean muscle, his skin porcelain and smooth. Tattoos cover his entirety from his neck to his torso, with swirling designs and creatures both real and mythical—most prominently, the black and scarlet snake coiled along his neck and chest. I would know since the man had been shirtless during our initial meeting.

No doubt about it, he's a work of art.

Today, the only visible tattoos are those on his hands, the rest are hidden beneath a crisp, tailored Brioni suit with a burgundy dress shirt.

He reaches up and runs his fingers through his perfectly coiffed raven hair - and it falls back to frame his face in an effortless yet deliberate way.

"How are we faring against death's grip?" he asks with a lightheartedness I can't fathom. For a man completely inked with tattoos, his demeanor is both beguilingly sophisticated and fittingly provocative, captivating, and raw all at once.

"That's your idea of waiting room talk?" I bristle, shifting uncomfortably in my seat. But I find myself inhaling deeply, wanting to savor the aroma that so completely envelops him: the sweet notes of smoldering sweet tobacco overlaid with exotic spices, permeating the air and lodging in my lungs.

"Death is all around us," He says glibly. "Why not talk about it?"

"Yeah, well, if my sister dies - it won't be from lack of a functioning heart." I remind him, my voice firm.

"Death is inevitable." he merely intones with a cryptic solemnity, "But it's also quite a fascinating thing. The moment something is born it is dying, yet it fights every moment of its life trying to resist its ultimate destiny. After all you have done, you understand that your sister will one day die anyway. So why do it at all?"

I want to cuss him out in defiance, his words are harsh and hardly befitting of the help he's given me but my words die in the air as he looks at me with those piercing eyes. So I still my anger; no use biting the hand that quite literally feeds me.

"Because that day is not today," I say coolly before taking a sip of my coffee to avoid having to say anything more.

I do my best to dismiss him by returning to my work, but his laughter that follows is low and ridiculously inviting, the sound of it dances on my spine, like someone slowly tracing their finger along it.

"Well said," he says with genuine admiration, a devilish grin, and the suggestion of humor in his voice that just won't quit.

Even if he's done a lot to help me in a really tough spot, he also has a screw loose. Who on earth is so brazenly insensitive?

I take a deep breath and ask him what I'm thinking: "Why are you here anyway? I thought you'd be done with me, since you already brokered the deal."

“I'm afraid it's just the opposite—I'll admit I'm a bit of a perfectionist. I always strive to be thorough,” he responds, "I need to ensure that my clients' desires are fulfilled. I wouldn't be doing my job properly if I didn't personally make sure the agreement is completed on both ends. My role is to see to it that you and your sister both get what you're due."

It's obvious he's got a certain something—a smooth sophistication matched with an otherworldly charm, when he wants to show it. But this is just business, so I give myself a mental slap to stay focused.

"Well then, thank you," I say finally, standing up from my chair and offering my hand for a shake.

He only stares at the gesture for a time before his gaze shifts away, to the paperwork I was half-heartedly engaged in. He makes no effort to take my hand, so I slowly allow it to drop by my side—iced by his nonchalance.

Damn, if you're prejudiced, just say that.

But, his tone is still seductively smooth as he speaks again with a polite air of acknowledgment: "Of course, the pleasure is all mine."

He reaches out and lifts one of the applications, his eyes scanning it quickly. "Helping the underprivileged meet their needs for housi ng...you're doing very important work here, Adora," he says, casting me a brief glance, before returning the application to the table and arranging them into a neat stack. "You're an industrious advocate for people who can't help themselves; believe me, it's truly a pleasure working with someone like you." He locks eyes with me then, and I hate that a little part of me swells up, like some love-struck schoolgirl getting attention from a crush.

"Or maybe you just have a soft spot for lost causes, hm?" he adds, unveiling his wolfish smile. And just like that, the man has gotten on my nerves all over again.

"I like to help people," I fire back, mustering up the little tolerance I have left for this conversation. "It's who I am."

He turns towards me and narrows his eyes, like he's daring me to challenge him. There's a spark of electricity that passes between us, and I can feel my heart racing as we lock eyes.

"Do you play chess, Adora?" he suddenly asks, catching me off guard.

Torn between confusion and a strange kind of anticipation, I bite my lip, and he follows the gesture.

Chess?

"A little."

And by that, I mean that I'm passingly familiar with the game. There was a time, growing up, when Alecia forced me into the neighborhood chess club for kids. I never had much patience for it, and I know now that it was mostly because ever since we lost our parents, she'd been all I had. She wanted to make sure I sowed friendships and commitments to social interests—even if it was chess club. They weren't my fondest memories, but they make the thought of losing Alecia all the more real.

"Show me then," He lays a hand softly atop my shoulder, and the instant his hand grazes me, my whole body jolts with energy. "Your sister is in capable hands, and you have a long wait ahead of you. Besides, your work will be here for you when you come back. At the very least, it will take your mind off things and make the time pass faster."

"And at the most?"

That gets a slight smile out of him, "Then you shall have someone to share your time with while they patch her up."

I hover hesitantly and can feel the objections building in my throat, but it's obvious that he knows me better than I'd hoped.

Guiding me to the doorway of the waiting room and pulling it open, he promises me softly, "I've already spoken with the staff. We'll only be a few doors down, and someone will come to get you the very instant surgery ends."

Clearly, Aviel has no intention of taking no for an answer and leaves me with no wiggle room. Once over the threshold, he strides wordlessly with confident and purposeful steps, simply expecting me to follow him, his footfalls reverberating off the walls of the long hallway.

The door seals closed behind us as he ushers me into a new, dark, and austere private room; a solitary chessboard table sits at its center. I can't help but wonder if this setup was prepared specifically for us two. Like other rooms in this clandestine operating facility, the walls are bare, the room itself stripped of most furniture or decoration. This place served only one purpose—and that was surgery. So, no need for anything else, really.

Aviel pulls out a seat for me in a gesture of meticulous courtesy, with a soft touch that raises goosebumps along my arms. I can feel his presence as he stands tall at my back, his energy radiating toward me. "Thanks," I say, my voice barely escaping my lips.

His obsidian gaze locks onto mine, and a muscle flexes in his chiseled jaw, his usually composed demeanor slowly tightens. The air around us thickens, and I swear he was just about to bend down to inhale my scent before taking a step back, and breaking the strange intensity between us.

I allow my gaze to wander along the coffin-like edges of the solid wooden board table as Aviel takes his position opposite me, the chessboard between us. He reaches down to grab the large wooden box beneath the table. His long fingers spread out over the lid and he opens it with gentle reverence, taking out each chess piece methodically.

"Put your phone away," He commands sternly. "You'll need to focus on the game and nothing else if you hope to win. I've never lost before." A ghost of a smile tugs at his lips as his gaze flicks towards me now and then while he arranges my pieces before me, and goes on, "You'll play black. Try your best."

"You're arrogant," I can't help but retort with a soft smile. His searing gaze follows me as I reluctantly turn my phone off and return it to my pocket, an ominous chill slithering up my spine. I had desperately wanted to check it, now I feel uneasy.

Aviel positions the rooks on the squared corners of his side of the chessboard. "Am I?" he murmurs, with a purse of his lips and a heavy gaze, a note of challenge worming its way into his tone. "We're about to find out—shall we make this interesting with a wager?"

"A wager?" I repeat, skeptical.

"Yes, you honor me by being my opponent—I feel obligated to reward you should you win." He draws closer and I catch a hint of something exotic on his breath that almost makes me dizzy. "What do you say?"

I'm hesitant, but intrigued—I invite him to go on, taking another sip of my coffee.

"If you win, I'll clear your two-hundred thousand dollar loan—no questions asked." He says, his voice a languid caress.

I nearly choke on my drink, and laugh at the absurdity of it. "C-can I get that in writing?" I splutter.

"If you don't take me at my word." He doesn't miss a beat. "But I promise, you won't need it." The double-entendre is not lost on me, something in me already expected he'd be expert at the backhand.

I frown, my anxiety deepening. "A-and if I lose?"

"Well, if I am victorious, you'll have to give me something I consider to be of equal value in return—nothing too extreme, naturally." His raised eyebrow almost dares me to accept.

Logic tells me not to accept this crazy proposition, I'm not the gambling type, I rarely even let my credit card expenditure go over thirty percent. But, right now I feel desperate. I know I'd be a fool to pass up the opportunity presented in front of me. I surprise myself by agreeing before I have the chance to change my mind. Hopefully, my few years of experience in chess club would prove useful here.

"I find chess is much like tragedy," Aviel utters slowly as he makes the opening move, savoring each syllable as though trying to convey more than the words themselves can ever express. "Both reveal so much about a person."

"I think the only thing it will reveal about me is that I'm a terrible player," I joke, attempting to lighten the atmosphere.

But Aviel's smile is tight.

He doesn't speak again until several moves later, intently watching my plays before he comments, "The Scandinavian Defense. Direct. Predictable. Not a terrible player, just a cautious one... which makes me wonder how you find yourself here in this place, participating in an illegal activity such as this."

I push forward one of my pawns and reply icily, "Don't you have a family...or anyone who matters to you?"

“No need to feel defensive, Adora, none of what I say comes with judgment—it's not my place.” he responds airily.

"It's not your place to ask either." I come to my next move and pause, Aviel's eyes are unwavering against mine.

"Would you rather I make another one of your pawns cry?" A smile teases the corner of his lips.

"Obviously not." I grimace, simultaneously berating myself for giving him such an obvious opening.

His smile widens and I'm sure my irritation is what draws it out of him. "You're right, but sometimes I like to indulge and you're making it hard not to," Aviel says. "To answer your question, I do have family, and yet they are more of a nuisance than anything else." He adds in a grim hiss and his expression turns wry.

I freeze as the tattoo on his hand catches my eye, I could have sworn I saw the centipede there move, and that the spider above it had been on his other hand just a day before. I rub my eye, I'm exhausted, my lack of sleep for the past twenty-four hours is probably getting to me. I clear my throat and meet his stare, finding that the gravity of his abyssal gaze seems to pull me into their void.

"You really find family a nuisance?" I ask, unable to look away.

"Isn't it? Your sister obviously set you on this path. You wouldn't be here if it weren't for her." His words are like another anchor on me, dragging me in further.

I manage to tear my eyes away and boldly drive a pawn forward.

"You're right, I wouldn't be here if it weren't for her," I whisper, but it's with admiration in my voice, and that seems to surprise him. "She practically raised me herself, and I can never thank her enough… she's everything to me." Immediately after saying that, I regret it—I didn't need to give him that information. But it's too late, like my pawn being swallowed alive by Aviel's own with an En Passant. Just another one of my many mistakes so far, I should have seen the feint.

*Okay, maybe chess **isn't** my thing.*

"And now you feel enslaved by those feelings for her? That she holds your soul in her hands? So much so that you find yourself doing something you never would have considered before?" He questions, arching a brow at me.

My annoyance grows as I attempt to downplay my blunder, "It is called love. Familiar with the concept?" I mentally pat myself on the back for capturing one of Aviel's knights just then.

"I am familiar..." He replies in a low tone, punctuating his words with a heavy pause, "...with fear, which is what people feel when they think they love someone. Fear to be alone or fear that no one will ever understand you as much as they do. Check."

The hairs on my arm stand as I reach out to shield my king, but simultaneously Aviel leans into the board, and for a moment I'm lost in confusion.

Until I feel it.

His finger skims across my knuckles, a mix of electricity and coldness shoots through my veins, and my heart is inexplicably sent racing in my chest.

My pawn is right there in front of me in my grasp, but I can't bring myself to move it. It feels like everything around us has stopped and suddenly a nightmare unfolds before me.

Time stops, gravity reverses and my whole world upends until I find myself pinned by an incomprehensible force to the tiled floor staring up into the ceiling, every muscle in my body straining against its invisible shackles. Fear and helplessness overwhelm me as I realize my sudden state of immobility, my only movements being my heaving chest and pounding heart.

Aviel slowly descends from above me like some dark angel and I can't look away, I'm transfixed by his hypnotic gaze, terror coursing through my veins as he extends his arm, a flood of thousand centipedes pouring out of his palm, writhing and scuttling over my body, their tiny legs tickling my skin despite the horror that freezes my muscles.

I want to scream for help, but my tongue is heavy in my mouth, any attempt to release a cry of help is futile. The pulsing darkness swells around me, pushing down on me like a great blanket. Tears spring to my eyes as the horrific creatures scurry over me, I can only close my eyes, surrendering to their touch.

Then, as quickly as the fear had been summoned, it's over—the spell is shattered and I'm right back where I had been moments before, clutching my pawn in a sweaty, shaking hand. Gasping for breath, I release my grip on the chess piece and scramble as far away from him as possible, toppling my chair with a clatter in the process. I stand still, feeling his touch linger on my skin as if he had never left and all I can do is tremble in the aftermath. My mind reels, blood roaring in my ears as I try to make sense of what has just happened.

From his seat opposite me, Aviel merely watches me with a distant, cool expression, as if he'd never been away.

"Wh-what the hell just happened?" My voice rasps through the air, echoing back to me in the oppressive silence of the room. "What did you do?"

"What do you mean?" He says, his gaze still embedded in mine. "Is this game proving to be more difficult than you thought?" He motions to the chessboard between us.

I shake my head in disbelief, my trembling finger pointing directly at him in accusation. "Y-y-you did something to me! There were insects — and it was you, I know it was!"

But he frowns and simply raises his hands as if to prove his innocence. "Relax." His voice is level and unemotional as if to emphasize his lack of guilt. "You need to breathe, Adora."

What I needed was to understand what had just happened. And, I had been breathing just fine!

"This is the liveliest I have seen you since you walked through my door," he chuckles and swiftly moved around to my side, lifting my chair upright once more, "Proving my theory once more that fear is what drives you all. Take a seat."

I'm afraid of many things, but at the top of that list is losing my sister. So whatever games he wanted to play, no matter what his plans are, I can handle him.

I take a deep, shaky breath and inch away from him before collapsing into my seat again if only because I'm not sure that my quivering legs can be trusted to stand. I'm compelled to know how he had done that, it suddenly crosses my mind that he might have drugged me with a hallucinogen.

I suspiciously eye my coffee cup, and see his lips curled into that elusive smirk, he watches my reactions with a predatory fascination. I decide not to risk anymore of the drink, and it's just as well, as though having read my mind, Aviel plucks it up from my side of the table and downs the rest of the coffee in a single swig.

"Instant. It figures you wouldn't appreciate it." he grimaces, "I apologize for that, I had hoped it would be freshly ground."

No drug then.

"Well," Aviel begins again, "Are you ready to continue?"

With two-hundred stacks on the line, I have no choice but to keep playing. I give a curt nod, and he grants an approving smile.

What motivated this man? I advance another piece on the board, wanting to understand him more.

Maybe I can find out.

"You helped me when no one else could, and you're here today when you don't have to be. So why exactly are you here? You say we're driven by fear—what drives *you*?"

"Careful, Adora, you are not as clever as you think you are," He warns, and deftly moves his king into the corner of the board, trapping mine in its wake. "Check."

My king scurries away to safety, but I can still feel his eyes focused on me as I protect it. I dare to look up at him again with newfound determination, despite feeling a looming trap. "Then educate me. What makes a man get into this line of business? If not to help people, then what?"

For a moment I feel as if he is peering into my soul, searching me for all my ills and vices.

"I enjoy seeing people being their most authentic selves," he replies.

"Circumstances drive people to your door, it doesn't mean that they're truly being themselves," I say. All I wanted was to save my sister and I wasn't about to become some kind of criminal because of this one experience.

"When the appropriate barriers are removed, one's true self is allowed to emerge. I am a remover of obstacles. There's no use in pretending with me, Adora, as I said before I do not judge," The way he says my name makes my pulse race and an electric current run through me. I've never been so captivated or so scared by someone. I've never met anyone like Aviel before, and I'm thankful for it.

"And, this is your most authentic self?" I ask before gesturing to his intimidating form.

Surprisingly, he lets out a laugh, one that lights up his face and makes his dark features come alive, his sharp canines glistening in the low light of the room.

"Yes," he says, bringing his rook forward with a hungry grin, "Checkmate."

Stunned, my gaze drops like lead to the chessboard on the tabletop. I hadn't seen it before, but now it's clear as day. I feel sick, like I'm waiting for the other shoe to drop, like the stakes might have been higher than I had realized.

I hear Aviel stand up, the chair legs scraping on the tiles, the isolated footfalls of polished dress shoes tapping against the floor as he makes his way around to close in on me. I still haven't looked up at him, too embarrassed by my own ignorance and naivety.

My heart thunders at his closeness, until his warm breath is sweetly mixing with mine in an intoxicating combination of spice and mint. He brings his lips close enough to my ear to graze my flesh as he murmurs with a voice that paralyzes me, "You are afraid."

I shudder involuntarily with his light touch and when I meet his gaze, I find a depth that I know will either be my salvation or my undoing.

"You're frightening," I admit honestly and he flashes those canines once more.

"You have no idea." he answers with a deep, throaty chuckle, though there is no underlying humor in his tone.

"The girl who told me about you said you aren't human," I offer.

He doesn't deny it, instead questioning me with a tilt of his head, "Is that so?" He moves to let his fingertips gently graze my jawline, he isn't accusing, merely asking.

I nod, my throat tight.

If he isn't human, then what is he?

He purses his lips as if thinking before finally answering my question with one of his own, "My being not-human isn't why you are afraid, is it?" His fingertips linger on my skin as if caressing and I feel my insides melt.

My heart lurches with the realization that he is right that I don't fear the unknown but rather what I know right now— that I am captivated by this man.

I flinch away from him and swallow hard, then close my eyes to compose myself before opening them back up to him. We need to get something straight, I am not a pushover.

"Fear isn't always bad—it's part of self-preservation," I reply before pressing my palm into the firm give of his broad chest, pushing him away with all the grace I can manage.

He takes a step back, affording me the distance I want and I can feel his mind working for a response, just as a saving grace ices over the air in the form of three knocks at the door.

We both freeze and glance toward the door in unison.

Aviel's expression gives way only fleetingly to his irritation, before he strides to the end of the room and throws wide open the door, revealing his assistant, John, and a doctor in the door frame, the latter announcing, "We did all we could."

I hold my breath.

"For now, it seems the surgery was successful." As the doctor speaks the words, my heart lifts with joy, my lips sliding back into a smile, and I clasp my hands together in gratitude.

"Thank you Dr. Apekos," Aviel turns to me with a tight smile, "It would seem we must put off the matter of my winnings for another time."

The hairs on my arms rise as he says this and then turns away, leaving me to ponder what lies ahead.

I follow the clinic's dull concrete walls and wan linoleum floors behind the surgeon this time. The only light comes from an occasional fluorescent pot light above, seemingly too sparsely placed to have any real effect, casting its eerie sheen across the environs.

Soon I'm ushered into Alecia's operating room, an almost blindingly bright, sterile white environment rife with medical equipment and devices. Complex diagrams and notes adorn the walls, while a faint scent of disinfectant lingers in the air, and a background hum of machinery fills the room.

The surgeon explains the arduous procedure that had been performed, that potent immunosuppressants were prescribed to ensure the heart would not reject, though Alecia, laying silent within the tight embrace of technology, would remain in a medically induced coma for some days to come, and due to the advanced state of her condition, her recovery would likely be a long and difficult one.

The doctor's voice fades to the back of my mind, where for a moment, I wonder with fear whether I've made the right decision for my sister.

My eyes trace the tubes that snake from her body, their ends plugged into the humming machines that form a half-circle around her bedside, maintaining her fragile life. Tears blur my vision as the surgeon continues speaking of payment and therapeutic services. Yet, all I can think of is Alecia– intubated and ventilated, and how she seems closer to death now more than ever.

The doctor excuses himself, leaving me to my thoughts in Alecia's room's quiet and cold stillness. It's then that I detect an unwelcome intrusion into my thoughts, inviting with it a frigid chill, and I nearly need a heart transplant myself as I hear the velvety voice of Aviel issue from directly beside me.

“You must admit,” he remarks. "She bears the pall of death gracefully." I hadn't heard nor seen Aviel's entrance, but here he was—side by side with me at Alecia's bedside.

I cut my eyes at him, and in a sharp tone, I retort, “I just want her to wake up and get better, so I can take her out of this place.”

"Well, you won't get far until her condition stabilizes," Aviel says almost teasingly, pointing to one of the machines beside Alecia's bedside.

I steel my body language, folding my arms across my chest. Not out of fear or intimidation but to create a literal divide between us—as if to push him away with all the might I can muster, however much he may have captivated me before.

“I only meant to say she looks peaceful,” In the corner of my eye, I see Aviel's expression soften into a faint smile. "Still, she may not be the same as she was before. The heart is a fragile thing, and rejection is always a risk—you know that."

I nod once. Of course, I know.

“And yet you went along with the decision anyway, even aware of the dangers.”

“It wasn't much of a decision—it was the only way to save her," I say, my words trembling from the weight of my conscience.

“We always have a choice, no matter how difficult. Pray tell, Adora," Aviel hums, his voice low and hypnotic. "What goes through your mind as you stand here, keeping watch over your sister's fragile body? What are your greatest apprehensions?"

I hesitate, uncertain if I want to share my innermost thoughts with this man. "Why should I answer you?" I finally give a cautious reply. I glance at Aviel, unsure of what he wants from me.

Aviel rewards me with a knowing, devilish smile—the kind that appears when one knows their prey more than they know themselves. "It's more for your benefit than mine," he says, "Expression is life; repression is suicide. If you let the words out, they'll have no power over you. Come now, tell me what's on your mind. Would it be so shameful? Or are your vocal cords muzzled by fear?"

I hadn't realized my lips were pressed shut, and my teeth gritted until Aviel had alluded to it.

I turn my eyes away, and in low earnest, I reply, hoping that vocalizing my worries would grant me at least a few moments of relief, "I’m afraid that the surgery will fail," I confide, my voice barely above a whisper. "That her body won't accept the new heart and I'll be responsible for her death."

"And those concerning yourself?" Aviel presses with intensity. "What is your greatest dread in all of this?"

"That I will never be able to forgive myself if something goes wrong," My breath catches in my throat, my heart racing faster than the machines beside the bed. "The guilt will eat me alive, and I'll never be able to move on from this."

Aviel nods, his gaze lingering on mine for a moment longer than necessary. "And yet, you still made the decision to go through with the procedure anyway. That takes a certain level of courage and conviction I find...fascinating."

I shiver at the way he said 'fascinating' as if I'm some sort of lab specimen. It was true though; I took a huge gamble at the risk of losing Alecia forever—for love, I'd said before, but that had been easier to say when I didn't have my sister lying here before me in this state.

"Now that you stand here in the aftermath, would you do it all again?" he asks, his voice a haunting melody to the backdrop of the monitors blinking and beeping in time with Alecia's weak pulse. I feel a cold knot form in the pit of my stomach, and Aviel leaves without another word, leaving me alone with only his question haunting me.

Alecia remained in a coma, hooked up to a host of machines that kept her alive. The nurses came and went, administering medication and checking her vitals, but there was no sign of improvement, and I could swear that she was getting worse. The nurses gave me the same response; they were doing all they could, and my patience was required. So, I sat by her side, watching over her, my mind awhirl.

Surprisingly, Aviel continued to stay by my side through my nightly visits. We'd occupy the two chairs by her bed; he offered no words of support, no words of kindness—yet still his presence became something I craved. He would silently keep me company through the long hours, simply waiting, or else engaging me in these conversations that led me to explore my thoughts and feelings in a way that made me question my own beliefs until there was nothing left for me to feel but a strange pull towards him.

I find myself growing increasingly dependent on his presence, both unsettling and somehow comforting in its own way, but above all, a steadfast and constant thing. He seemed to understand my fears and doubts in a way that no one else did, as he said, without judgment, seeming to breathe in my anxieties and worries to leave only a void of stillness, during which I could ease my mind and still my racing heart.

"What are your morals, Adora?" he asks me one night as we sit in the hospital room, hours after the sun dipped below the horizon.

"What do you mean?" I ask, but he doesn't turn to glance at me.

"How do you justify the fact that someone died for your sister to live?"

I look at Alecia, her chest rising and falling beneath the thin blanket. "I can't answer that," I say solemnly, my gaze never leaving her. "I don't have time to question what might have happened, only to make the best of what I have. Right now, all I have is Alecia."

A silent moment passes between us before he finally speaks again. "So you sacrifice feelings to protect feelings?" He muses.

"It's not like that." I feel a tightness constricting my throat. "I would have done anything to save her."

He briefly considers my words before continuing, "You would die for her?"

"Of course," I whisper without hesitation.

"What will you do if she never wakes up?" he asks softly.

His question startles me and causes my heart to sink like a stone in my chest. The thought of Alecia never waking up again is too agonizing to bear.

"I don't know," I manage quietly, feeling the thick weight of uncertainty and sorrow on my chest.

“What will you do if the operation takes her life?” he probes further, his midnight eyes drilling into mine.

My mind races with the thought of losing my only family. How would I go on if I lost her? I swallow hard, trying to block out the terrifying answer that swims in my head.

I'd follow her.

I want to disappear in that moment; his question too honest, too raw. All I can manage to muster is a feeble and vague reply: “I'll still love her, even when she's gone."

Aviel nods, but I know he sees through my platitude. "Perhaps your notions of love and loyalty are more powerful than anyone can ever master or control. Still," he says without emotion, "The correct answer is to grieve and accept the choice you made for her."

My heart aches in that moment, and I desperately need a distraction. "So, what would you have wanted for winning our chess game?" I ask, aching to steer our conversation away from her, hoping he wouldn't push further into this matter any longer than necessary.

His alluring smile is a ruse as he utters, "The correct thing to do is not bring it up."

"I'm curious."

"About me?"

I nod. "I guess what I'm asking is what a man like you would possibly want," I say, intrigued by how his eyes seem to dance with a secret.

"You mean what I would take..." He whispers. "Before it would have been the hope that burned against its own extinction. And now..." Aviel's response ends there, and he simply shrugs. He leaves me entranced yet wary of his unknown intentions.

I follow him with my eyes as he rises and towers over me, the menacing aura emanating from him sending a chill down my spine. I swallow down the fear that threatens to rise in my throat.

Softly, he asks, "I wonder, if your sister recovers, will you finally let go of your curiosity of me?" His words send a wave of heat across my face, and there's something in his tone that makes me feel like I'm standing on the edge of a cliff with no idea of what's below.

I meet his gaze fiercely as I retort, "You're just as fascinated with me," indicating the odd fact that he never left my side. "Otherwise, why would you be here? Your part to play finished days ago." I counter. "But here you are."

He steps back as though just seeing me for the first time and takes a deep sigh before looking at me with a faint smile that doesn't reach his eyes. "Perhaps I have allowed this go on for long enough," he says more to himself than anyone.

Decidedly, Aviel gathers his coat from his chair, folding it over one arm. He plants a hand on my shoulder, locking his gaze with mine for a long moment, "Have a goodnight, Adora." he finally says, then slowly strides out of the room.

I sit alone by Alecia's bedside, reliving his words as my eyelids closed and I drift off into a dreamless sleep.

A deafening beep suddenly jolts me from my slumber, and I freeze, stunned. The constant beep of the machine that monitors Alecia's vital signs suddenly changes in pitch.

I leap from my chair, and my haze of drowsiness instantly turns to panic. I nearly fall on top of her bed trying to press the button to call for the doctor, as her vitals shift to a faster and stronger pulse, and as Alecia begins to stir, I tighten my grip on the bed rails. My heart surges with anticipation as Alecia's eyelashes flutter and her eyes slowly open. I never take my eyes off of her even as the doctor files into the room, followed by both Aviel and John.

“Hey,” Alecia murmurs, her voice raw from the ordeal, her gaze meeting mine.

“Hey back,” I reply, barely managing to utter the words choked with emotion. “How are you feeling?”

“Like someone gouged my heart out.” She jokes weakly, wincing as she tries to reposition herself in the medical bed.

"At least you'll get a cool scar out of it." I smile with bleary eyes and clasp her hand in mine and give a firm squeeze, though she can barely return it.

If I were a religious person, I'd be tempted to offer up a prayer of thanks for Alecia's recovery, but I know better than to look for divine intervention here. It was the shady connections of Aviel – that mysterious figure lingering in the shadows – who had brought about this miracle.

And Aviel didn't appear like someone to ever pray to.

The doctor swiftly fills my place beside Alecia to examine her, and so I glance towards Aviel, I notice a flicker of dissatisfaction in his eyes, as they meet mine—a sign that our convoluted dance is far from over.

"Here you go," I beam, presenting a tray of heart-healthy food to Alecia and setting it on her lap, only to watch her eyes widen with horror at the sight of my breakfast creation.

"You can't be serious," she says. "This isn't food; it's punishment."

I raise my hands defensively and try to keep the laughter out of my voice. "Hey, I worked hard on it. It'll give you plenty of energy to start your day."

Alecia and my sad egg-white scramble and oatmeal with almond milk stare one another down.

"At least it's seasoned." I offer. "And it's better than what you got at the hospital."

Alecia groans, "Come on, I can't get an egg and biscuits? A *half* of a doughnut? Damn, a latte?"

I fling open the curtains, letting the morning sun rays flood the room, then plop down at the foot of her bed with a chuckle. "That *is* egg. It's not that bad."

"Cap," Alecia says, pointing her fork at me.

"Remember what you used to tell me? I'm not making anything else; it's this or nothing." I say, "You should be happy to hear you were right all along."

Alecia sighs, "Damn, my words of wisdom." She takes a few hearty bites of my cooking, which she comments isn't bad, and washes it down with a large glass of orange juice and her medication.

A private nurse's aide came in to teach me how to check Alecia's vitals and general care for the first couple of days back from the clinic. They also left us with their personal number but insisted we call an ambulance in case of an emergency. Appointments were also scheduled to see how Alecia's recovery is coming along. Aviel's people had seen to everything.

He hadn't left my mind since the day Alecia and I left the clinic, but I hadn't seen him again since. Somewhere between his mercurial nature and foreboding presence, Aviel had become a fixture of fascination in my mind.

But I quickly shake my head, pushing away these thoughts—I need to pay attention to Alecia and her recovery. And to refocus, I take out a few get-well cards and presents addressed to Alecia from various sources—friends, and neighbors alike.

Helen and Tayo had visited and brought with them get-well cards and a bouquet with the stems cut. The flowers are assembled in a giant mason jar, filled to the brim with beautiful, colorful blossoms, and sit on the dresser, injecting some life into the otherwise barren room.

The need to pay off our debt drove me to desperate measures, and I ended up selling what possessions I could; electronics, jewelry, and the few designer handbags we'd collected over the years. I also took up more hours at the office. Along with the rest of our joint savings, our combined credit, what I could borrow on such short notice, and a loan from my workplace, the debt was being widdled down to a manageable number.

I rise from my seat on the bed and situate another pillow behind her back, "Try to do your exercises while I'm gone; the nurse said ten minutes, then a short walk if you can manage it."

"Ugh, I was hoping to just sleep in when you went to work." Alecia plays it off as a joke, but as with any other patient, Alecia is not immune to the consequences of recovering from physical trauma. She's been like this since she came home from the clinic, weak, lightheaded, and prone to bursts of extreme fatigue so severe that she can only sit in bed during the day.

"Uh-uh, you're not sleeping in until you do what the nurse said," I tell her, "Call me if you need to, and if you don't feel well, call the nurse before you call me."

I watch Alecia painstakingly fight to finish a few more bites, and although she's only managed to eat a few morsels, I am happy that it's more than she had yesterday, but I wonder how she can subsist on so little.

After giving her one last chance to fill that empty void, reluctantly, I reach for the tray to take it away. She turns to face me with a pained smile and whispers: "Look at us. I'm your big sister; I'm supposed to be the one taking care of you..."

"No ma'am," I say firmly, stacking the dishes atop one another. "You've taken care of me my whole life. Now it's my turn."

A somber silence hangs in the air as Alecia gazes into nothingness. "Adora," she begins suddenly.

I can feel a lump in my throat slowly growing, but I remain silent.

Alecia ventures, "Something's been on my mind..."

Knowing all too well where this is going, I feel my stomach drop to my feet and hurry to leave. "I'm late; we can talk after work—"

"Adora," Alecia grabs my wrist and fixes me with a hard stare. "How did you manage to get me a heart transplant?"

The tension in the room is thick and heavy. I don't want to tell Alecia the truth, but I know I can't keep it from her forever.

"I took out a loan," I mumble, avoiding my sister's piercing gaze. She tenses up, waiting for more of an explanation.

"A loan?" Alecia repeats with confusion, "A loan won't buy you a heart...I was on a waiting list—"

"And I got you off of it," I cut her off, gathering the courage to say what I've been avoiding all this time, "—and pushed to the front of the line."

Another long beat of silence follows as Alecia waits for me to go on. When she sees that I'm not going to, she says: "Tell me how. Did you have to...do something to get me on the top of the list?"

I swallow hard as her question hangs in the air between us, which thickens with anticipation. Knowing she won't let it go until she gets an answer, I slowly nod my head in confirmation and then do my best to reassure her, "Don't worry; it's not like I offed anyone. I took out a loan with the help of a man named Aviel, who said he could get the job done, and he got it done."

Before Alecia can plead for more information, I go on, grasping desperately onto any excuse to avoid further questions, "You need to rest; you can't be stressing yourself out like this." I grab my keys and take my purse off of the nightstand next to her bed.

I manage to pull myself away from this moment of vulnerability and offer an answer with false finality. "I took out a loan. It was a big one. That's all."

"Okay, okay...just one more question," Alecia says cautiously. "I just need to know...how much?"

Taking a deep breath, I stop for a moment and exhale. It's not like she wouldn't find out eventually, anyway. "Two hundred grand."

Alecia's face transforms into shock only briefly, but she manages to school her features back into concerned love; she whispers, "That's too much-"

I shake my head quickly, "It's not. It was worth it." I say firmly.

Alecia didn't know that I had spent every night lying awake, staring at the ceiling, wondering how I would repay the loan, but never once did I ever regret it. The money meant nothing compared to her life.

"I would have rathered that you got the life insurance money and invested it..." Alecia starts, but I know her heart isn't in this scold.

"No, you wouldn't," I say definitively, slinging my purse over my shoulder and taking a step toward the door. "I wouldn't either."

I know what she's thinking, and I can't blame her. If the roles were reversed, all of the same thoughts would have run through my head too.

She looks up at me with a determined gaze. "We'll figure this out together. I'll get better soon and get a new job when I'm out of this damned bed."

My heart pulses with love for my sister. I've never felt so grateful for anything in my life, but I don't have it in me to tell her that I only have a few short days before the lenders expect my payment in full.

Aviel

♥

"Aviel?..."

I can feel my fingers flexing and unflexing as I step closer to the floor-to-ceiling window of my home office, trying to hold onto the image of Adora in my mind as it fades away into the nebulous white of the swirling snowfall.

***

"Adora!-" I called out, never more desperate to have someone stop in their tracks, and not quite knowing why I felt so compelled to say her name at all, why I hung on the sound of it in my mouth when it had left my lips and why I hadn't simply glanced at her and said nothing, averting my eyes from her face.

She stopped in her tracks at the sound of my voice and turned around slowly to face me. Her eyes darted between me and her sister being helped into the vehicle, trying to gauge my motive for calling her out.

My frame stood rigid, my fists clenched at my sides as the tension between us thickened.

"Yes?" she eventually replied, her voice barely louder than a whisper, though it felt like a shout in the eerie silence. Her fingers dug into the door frame, clutching it like a lifeline, while her other hand trembled slightly.

For a few seconds, neither of us moved or said a word as we locked eyes with one another like two magnets unable to tear our gazes away from each other.

I eventually broke the silence.

"I wanted to apologize for my earlier behavior during our chess match," I said, neither raising nor lowering my voice but instead maintaining its unwavering presence. "I fear it was unbecoming of me."

After a few moments of silence, Adora took a deep breath and finally nodded her tear-stained face in agreement. "See," she started, with something close to a smile. "You fear too."

I'd expected a groveling thank you.

I could never admit to the dismay she had caused within me with that simple statement. I mustered a sneer at that, but for a moment, something in me slipped, and I couldn't stop the small laugh that escaped my lips, and Adora's faint smile spoke volumes.

"I thought about your question, and I'd go through this a hundred times if it meant saving my sister again and again. That's love." She said before turning away from me to make her way out the door, never looking back again.

***

"Aviel, sir?" My assistant, Jame's, voice comes again, soft yet persistent, wanting to get my attention without startling me—which does little to stop him from annoying me.

My flesh is tight with restless energy as the tattoos on my body begin to stir restlessly on the surface of my skin, writhing along my wrists and shifting along my biceps, shoulders, and chest. I slow and deepen my breaths in an attempt to quell their movement.

Jack is successful when he speaks again. "Sir?"

It's enough to bring me out of the seclusion of my mind. My gaze snaps to him in warning, still feeling tense and irritable. "What is it?" I hiss sharply through clenched teeth.

My aide is not a short man, yet he seems to shrink into his charcoal gray suit when I set my glare upon him. I can see his Adam's apple bob as he begins again. "It's two o'clock. You have an appointment." He reminds me, turning his tablet around to reveal my daily schedule.

My stare lingers on his a while longer before I look down at the screen. A deep exhale leaves my nose, and I roll my eyes in disdain, attempting to soothe my suddenly sour mood.

But just then, Adora's face flashes intrusively through my mind, and I can almost feel her presence. Anger boils within me—I want nothing more than to have her here before me just one more time, but then I'm disturbed that she should even be on my mind at all. She is just a woman. Just a human. Something I want to forget, and yet...

With my servant standing before me, I feel all the more shackled to a life of obligations and expectations. I have no appetite to deal with another groveling human right now, not when Adora has been consuming my thoughts in the recent days.

She thought she had won, and I'd seen the look of anticipation on her face as her hands grasped the bed rails and unshed tears brimmed in her deep brown eyes before cascading down her cheeks when her sister finally opened her eyes in her bed.

Was that love? They had nothing except debt and each other, yet they somehow managed to seem content with their shared fate.

The look of joy and tears that crossed Adora's face was almost unbearable to witness. It was just as intense as her fear and inexplicably mesmerizing, filling me with a powerful and unwelcome wave of sensation, rushing through me for a fleeting moment. Such a vulnerable display of emotion was...

My lip curls with distaste at the memory.

Pathetic.

Torn between pity, disgust, and scorn, I'd arranged for her and her sister to be taken home and far away from my presence.

"Sir?" Joseph's voice breaks through my thoughts. The look on his face is somewhere between fear and mild impatience. "Something on your mind—you seem distracted. Is it that woman?" Jerald asks.

“You remember what I said about personal conversations?" I remind him. "Ask me what’s on my mind, and you won’t like what you find.” I spit. I dismiss my annoying servant, letting him know I will take the appointment, and watch the man disappear, but not before his relief is made plain.

I know my assistant resents me, and I don't blame him. I would too, if I were him. I'm sure I wouldn’t tolerate the ills of a cruel, cold, dictatorial employer, but if he does his job, it doesn't matter. Plus, he's paid well enough.

I live for striking deals with humans and collecting their souls when they undoubtedly fail to pay up, and it has never once felt like a chore until today. I hate that Adora enthuses me more than witnessing another human entrap themself. That's why I hasten through the appointment as quickly as possible, just so I can return to thoughts of her, wondering if she could be right.

The logical side of me refuses her words. Still, another part of me wonders if I have lingered on the earth long enough to see the consequences of my actions finally start to manifest in the form of this insidious pull that's taken root in me. I remember my father's words when I declared my freedom, he promised that I would come to regret my rebellion one day; was this it? I refuse to believe that, nor will I ever accept it.

As if sensing my distress, Lilith stirs from her repose on the cushion across the room and slithers towards me.

"What do you think, old friend?" I ask her gravely.

Her eyes glint like jewels, as striking as they had been when she was human—my very first contract with a woman who loved too well and lost too much, the first woman who loved the first man. She had foolishly thought she could capture his heart and failed miserably, her love forever doomed to be unrequited. And now she remains by my side in servitude, part of me forever. At the very least, I had helped her to enact the revenge she so deserved. And, she had followed me, along with all my other contracts, when I left my father and the abyssal realm behind - all those souls stolen from him and now a part of me as well.

"You have loved before; was it worth it?" Her scales are cool beneath my touch, and she lets out a satisfied hiss.

Of course, she would agree with the human sentiment - above all else; they always pined for something - only to be met with more unfulfilled longing. Fueled by fear, avarice, arrogance and acrimony, and every other awful emotion that led them to crave more than they had, forever unsatisfied—yet it was I who garnered the title of evil? Ridiculous.

"Come, let's take a short visit," I declare, lifting her onto my shoulders; Lilith encircles me, lustrous against the dark fabric of my shirt. "Perhaps if the sister's heart has failed, you can have it." I get a narrow-eyed, accusatory glare for my effort and merely scoff at her inability to take a joke.

Lilith may be my companion, but Adora has taken something from me that I never expected—my peace of mind. She aroused a foreign sensation within me, something the likes of which I had never experienced so aptly before. Was it dread? Loathing? No, neither seemed to fit.

She stirred within me something far more powerful and passionate.

It's a long drive to Adora's apartment. I ignore Jude's obvious glances at me in the rearview—it is abnormal for me to visit a client before a deadline, but I offer no explanation, and he's smart enough not to ask. The tires sing a song of anticipation as we turn down the street filled with bare frosted trees casting shadows on the pavement outside of Adora's apartment complex. I instruct him to keep the car running until my return.

I stroll up the path, eyeing a small parcel left at the entrance, then fist my knuckles against the door of her ground-floor apartment, and after a few moments, I can hear faint noises echoing from within before her voice peeps out tentatively, slightly muffled behind it: "Who is it?"

She must be alone with her sister. "Open the door, Adora," I say without pause.

Silence follows before she inquires again, "What do you want?"

Holding back my frustration at her audacity is difficult, but I reply as coolly as I can through gritted teeth. "I will tell you when you open the door."

"I'm busy. Come back later."

The insufferable woman makes my jaw clench tighter. I pluck the parcel up from her doorstep, coming upon an idea. "Too bad," I smirk. "I have a package for you."

"Go away. I'll pick it up after."

I lean into the door, and in a low and husky voice, I threaten, "If you want what's yours, you know what to do. If not, I'll be taking this rubbish back with me."

The sound of the deadbolt unlocking and the chain sliding off resonates in my ears. Finally, the lock disengages in a thin click before she yanks open the door. Adora snatches the box from my waiting hands without missing a beat and jumps back with a strangled shriek as Lilith uncoils around my neck and strikes at the air with a hiss. The box tumbles from her grasp to the ground.

I knew from the start that the shock on Adora's face when she opened the door would be worth it. Her terror due to Lilith's presence only heightens the moment. My body tenses with joy as I savor it. Serves her right for making me wait.

"T-there's a fucking snake around your neck!" she manages to stammer, her voice both high and strained.

I bend at the knee and retrieve the parcel, tucking it under my arm again. I suppose I can't trust her to hold anything right now, not with the way she's trembling.

"Thank-you, I really hadn't noticed," I purr out in response and sip in the sight of her. Adora's deep brown eyes rove between me and my companion, unsure of what is happening.

Unable to resist the temptation any longer, I take a step closer, the soles of my shoes barely making a sound against the floorboards. However, Adora remains rigid, and her breath audibly hitches as she decides whether we should be here or not.

That won't do at all.

A sinuous smile curves my lips as I tilt my head and let my gaze burn on her before my polite inquiry slips from me: "May we come in?"

I know that when I'm this close, human inhibitions weaken, so while it should be evident that we are both welcome, it seems Adora could use some help this one time. Again, her gaze flits between my face and that of my familiar while I wait patiently for an answer. Her lips part, her chest heaves, and she finally cedes to my request and accepts our entry.

"Shit, you've got some nerve," Adora scoffs and runs a hand through her cropped hair, looking more alluring than ever before. Without thinking, I can feel my fingers twitch against the urge to touch her soft-looking hair. "You know, you could've told me you were coming."

I give her my most charming slow smile. "And, would you have opened the door then?"

She doesn't answer, of course.

"I thought so." I chuckle and offer her the package again. "Slowly this time," I say, leaning toward her, "Or you'll frighten Lilith again."

She gingerly reaches out and accepts the box. In an instant, something sparks between the two of us, and the tension dissipates, leaving only an inexplicably captivating emotion to hang in the air.

Adora moves to lock the door behind us all and turns around, disappearing further into her apartment; I follow after her scent like an addict.

"So, you're making house calls too now?" She says more light-hearted now, but she tugs at her clothes in an attempt to look more put together, and it may have worked if I couldn't see through her facade. "I'm surprised." She plants a hand on her hip.

"Just this once." My eyes roam around, slowly absorbing the modest comforts of her abode. It's a studio apartment with recycled wood floors offset by white walls and taupe accents, and kept in good order.

It seems to be in decent repair, but it's definitely not the home of someone who could readily afford the debt she just accrued. There's a marked minimalism, but then again, she had made a deal with me—it likely resulted from selling what she could.

"Lilith was eager for a visit anyway," I reply, setting Lilith down so she can explore the apartment. Adora's eyes widen, and she yanks a foot up off the floor, just out of the path of the glinting red scales and the smooth, fluid movements of the serpent.

"Lilith? That's really her name?" She asks, training her eyes on Lilith, who is exploring and cataloging every corner of the small apartment with a serpent's precision. "She looks like a Lilith." Adora seems just as fearful as she is mesmerized by her beauty.

"She was named such because she so readily embodies the spirit," I explain. I can tell she doesn't quite understand, but she nods anyway.

We arrive in a petite kitchen where I take a seat at the bar, allowing my eyes to rove over the vicinity; the counters are clean but cluttered with doilies, pink and red cards, heart cut-outs, and various other crafting scraps.

"I wasn't expecting company," Adora opens the refrigerator to retrieve a pitcher of water, giving me a view of the numerous pink and red cards plastered to the door.

"Do tell, what's the occasion? Are you having a soiree?" I drawl, my eyes sliding over all of the decorations. As she steps forward to set a cold glass of water in front of me, I capture her stare and hold it.

Her gaze shifts away from mine in a painfully obvious manner. "It's Valentine's Day tomorrow," she mutters, indicating that I am to accept this as explanation enough, then moves to the refrigerator to replace the pitcher inside, her back turned to me.

I reach for a hand-crafted paper heart atop the counter, holding it between two fingers, I turn it over in my hand, and read the words scrawled on its surface, “Happy Single Losers Day?”

I barely get the sentence out of my mouth before she whips around, then she lunges instinctively, but I snatch it away beyond her reach. Adora is in my space in an instant, her delicate frame pressing against mine as she tries to grab the paper from my possession.

“Give it!” Her breath is hot on my neck; something in me revels at her nearness.

I offer an olive branch and release my grip, and she manages to reclaim it, but my smile is only met with her stern glare as she clutches the heart to her heaving chest and struggles to regain her composure.

I merely allow the silence to hang in the air, an eyebrow subtly lifting to coax out her further elaboration.

“It’s Alecia’s—it's both of our favorite holiday," She slides her eyes away from me. Expecting me to scorn her suggestion, her voice trails off. "And, I want to do something cheesy and nice for her—especially this year...”

She assumes I’ll sneer, so I satisfy her expectations.

My amused chuckle fills the air as I take a slow sip of water, savoring her flinch as I do so. “You are mad,” I reply, baring my teeth in a grin and enjoying how she squirms beneath my heavy gaze.

"You need to lighten up," she scowls at me, scraping up the rest of the decorations and throwing me a fiery look that would have melted my heart had I had one. Her next words come sharply. "What are you even doing here anyway?”

"How is Alecia faring?" I parry back smoothly with a question of my own.

Adora takes a deep breath before responding hesitantly, "She's okay," before adding, "Better. She still needs a lot of rest though; she's sleeping."

"Ah..." I reply silkily, "I was hoping for more stimulating news—like how she is starting to behave like the murderer we snatched that heart from."

Adora's eyes widen in shock and revulsion—her full lips parted in horror—and I can't help but take pleasure in her expression. The decorations drop from her arms where she stands.

"Please tell me that's some twisted joke," she says, her voice barely audible.

"It was one of my best..." My voice trails off as I take one last sip from my glass before setting it aside, standing up to retrieve the paper hearts from the tiles, and setting them back on the counter. I rise to my full height and lock eyes with her—the air around us charged with unexpected electricity.

She breathes a sigh of relief, then smacks my chest in a half-reprimanding way. "Well, don't do that again."

Inexplicably, a smile tilts the corner of my lips. My hands reach out for hers, a thrill rushes through me as the tips of my fingers lightly graze them before taking her hands into my own. I peer down at her—and I can't help but bring her closer to whisper in her ear. "Look who needs to lighten up."

Her hands tremble in my hold, and I feel her temperature rise several degrees with each harsh breath she takes, betraying both fear and arousal at my innocent touch. The heat between us is palpable as I edge her body against the counter, our eyes locked together.

"You and I have unfinished business, Adora." I utter, barely above a whisper, "There's still the matter of what I've won."

Adora's eyes widen in shock. A warmth spreads through my veins as a sweet scent emanates from her skin—lust, but something else too—something...better.

"I'd forgotten," she whispers breathlessly.

Still holding her gaze with mine, I move in, my fingers lightly grazing her jawline, causing her to shiver with anticipation. "I didn't." I say softly, "Now that the matter of your sister is an obstacle removed, what do you want?" I urge in a soothing whisper. "Tell me what it is you fear so much now."

Adora bites into her full lower lip, and suddenly, it stops being about what she wants. It's about what I want and what I am going to take.

My body moves before my brain has time to process it, feeling the magnetic force between us. I engulf her lips with mine, capturing her gasp of surprise, desperate to consume her essence. Our tongues entwine in a passionate dance, and her taste is like an ambrosia dripping from the heavens, an unearthly sweetness that fills me with a warmth I have never before experienced. I suck her tongue to draw every last bit of that sweetness.

I bit my lip, breaching the flesh so that a drop of my life force mixes into the kiss; she shudders beneath me, her defenses crumbling and her arousal filling the air as the answer to what her true is desire emerges — me. She wants me like no other, and I want nothing more than to be deeply enmeshed in her.

Finally, I pull away from her lips, leaving her breathing harsh, and savor my way up her neck, my lips never leaving her skin, feeling every contour of her skin and leaving a trail of fiery kisses in their wake.

She quivers beneath my touch and releases a faint moan when I drag my tongue along the dip in her clavicle until, finally, Adora throws her head back in ecstasy while giving me full access.

I reach a hand for Lilith, and she joins us, letting me guide her to Adora's wrists. Adora startles for a moment as Lilith secures her about the arms, her sharp inhale reverberating in the air, but my abrasive kisses are enough to distract her. When I rip her shirt open, and my lips descend to the swell of her breast to draw her peaks into my mouth, she is writhing, submerged in pleasure. Helplessly enthralled, I have her teetering at the edge of rapture, completely at my mercy.

"I'm going to make you come, and you're going to let me," I growl against her ear, drawing out the promise like a forbidden secret between us.

She tips her chin in a nod. A primal hunger courses through my veins as I look upon this tantalizing creature before me, and I scoop her up and set her atop one of the kitchen bar stools. Her hips were now aligned with mine, at the perfect height for me to ravage her body. The temptation of her is overwhelming, but I haven't fucked a human in decades, and I'm not sure I want to now—the desire pouring out of her now is more than enough satisfaction for me for now, and I breathe it all in.

Roughly, I unbutton her jeans and tenderly cup her throbbing center through her slick underwear, she melts into my touch, spurring me on. I let my thumb draw agonizing circles around her most sensitive spot, coaxing her to arch into my every movement. She throws her head back in ecstasy, wanting more. And I give it to her.

Her breath hitches, and she moans my name, shattering any last restraint I have. My speed and intensity increase as I press my face into her neck and breathe in her captivating aroma, her scent intoxicating me, and my appetite for her untameable.

"You will come for me," I rasp, my own voice sounding alien to my ears.

I sense something within me stirring; I can feel it, waking after a long slumber. I feel my old self emerging beneath its human mask, exposing my true nature. There is nothing I can do to stop it. Before I know what I am doing, I sink my fangs into her skin just as she reaches completion. Her entire body vibrates with pleasure, and I taste it in her blood. It's heavenly, far more than anything I'd indulged in decades ago.

I tear myself away from her abruptly, the reality of what I've just done hitting me full force. I step back and curse at myself, turning from her—what madness has brought me here with this human?

"Aviel?" her trembling voice hits my senses, filling the air with a sweetly seductive melody, and brings me to round on her and face her enthralling beauty.

She gasps sharply at my appearance and jerks back, her fear heightening with each passing moment, and I feel my tattoos coming savagely alive, rippling and lashing their excitement for the mix of emotions we elicit from her. My arousal only heightens. Her fear, combined with all her other emotions is an aphrodisiac like no other, but my blood in her must be helping her calm down because her desire still overrules her apprehension.

Growling, I take her by the hair, dragging her towards me and crushing her lips against mine hungrily. She returns my passion ounce for ounce, and when I push her to her knees, she greets it unresistingly.

I slide my fingers to my belt buckle and release myself from my pants. My voice rumbles darkly, dripping with yearning, as I lock her gaze with mine: "Take me into your mouth."

She opens up, and with her hands bound behind her, I feed myself to her, pushing past her supple lips. She looks so tempting on her knees like this, her mouth full of my cock. But it's not enough. Finally, I thrust myself in, and she struggles with my size, but I keep her there, on her knees, mouth full of my manhood and my hand clutching the back of her head. I bask in the sensation of her warm tongue caressing my shaft, and the tight depth as she hollows her cheeks and draws me in with her suction.

I want to keep her like this, ready for me whenever I want her. I push deeper and deeper, gradually increasing the speed of my thrusts, desperately trying to keep from succumbing to the agonizing pleasure too soon. My blood boils, and I have to bite my lip hard to stop the roar the threatens to breach the base of my throat.

I throb within her, searching for respite from this madness. She moans, her throat vibrating pleasure all the way up my length. The intense heat of my blood runs down my chin, at the same time the slickness of my desire seeps from my member as her tongue encourages me to let go of all control. I can't hold my groans back any longer.

Ahhh, her mouth, her sweet mouth...this woman... Fuck! Even with the limited movement she has now, she's voracious.

I want this moment to last forever, as I am drenched in the sensations only she can give me. Finally, I let go of my control, surging into her one last time and taking me over the edge with unbelievable force. I grunt, feeling immense satisfaction as she swallows every drop I give her. Gently disengaging from her embrace, I graze a tender thumb across her wet lips as I peer down into her eyes.

"This moment captures your soul's truest form," I say in a hushed whisper, my desire still coursing through me.

The fog of passion veiling her gaze evaporates, and her eyes turn to steel. "Let me go."

Lilith uncoils herself from Adora's arms, while I recompose myself, and I'm not even done zipping my pants when Adora thrusts her finger at the door.

"Leave." she commands.

"You can't possibly be angry at me for giving you an orgasm?"

Before I could say another word, she shoves me towards the door. "You've taken your prize, haven't you?"

"I'm not done with you." I move to take a step closer, but she's not having it.

"You know where the door is!" Her voice is cold and uncompromising. But her gaze speaks more than words, exposing a deeper feeling she has for me.

Regret.

What we've done has made her regretful...

I feel a pang of...*something.*

My limbs seem to freeze, something about her expression makes me want to drop to my knees, yet my pride keeps me on my feet, enraged that the thought even crossed my mind.

With lingering heat in my veins, I lower myself to retrieve Lilith as she approaches, then stride to the door and Adora doesn't even give me a chance to say anything else before slamming it in my face.

I feel a deep emptiness, like something crucial has been suddenly taken away, as if I'm missing something.

My mind blanks as I return to the vehicle, Jeff is puzzled at my demeanor, and I note the way his gaze lingers questioningly on my bloody lip; nonetheless, he drives us back to my residence without comment. I wouldn't have heard him even if he did say anything; all that fills my mind is Adora...

Humans, so frustrating. But two can play this game, and I'm going to give her one hell of a gift tomorrow.

"This is so sad and so brilliant at the same time." Alecia laughs from across the room as she reads through the collection of messages I've written, picking through the pile of heart-shaped cards strewn across the coffee table. As she flips through them, the soft sound of her mirth echoes in my ears.

I can't help the grin plastered on my face, thankful for my sister and our yearly tradition.

It's a stark contrast to the terrors that linger in the recesses of my mind. Last night, I was plagued by a series of nightmares, the only one I can remember being about Alecia in a hospital bed struggling for life, hooked up to machines and tubes, her body frail and weak. Beneath the sheets where my sister lay, blood was soaking through the covers at her chest.

I frantically looked around the hospital room to find no one there; doctors who should have been helping were nowhere to be seen. Pure dread and desperation mingled with the sterile scent in the air; my pleas for help unheard and unanswered.

I had woken up hyperventilating and nearly tripped over my feet to get to Alecia's room, only to find she was still there, and safe. She slept peacefully while I trembled and gasped like a fish out of water, sinking to my knees on the floor beside her bed.

Pushing the memory from my mind, I return to the living room with the freshly iced, slightly lop-sided Valentine's Day cake I baked myself. I didn't even bother opening the package with a heart-shaped cake mold that arrived yesterday, but that didn't matter now.

I set the cake down on the coffee table—ugly as it is, it still tastes good.

Alecia pressed her hand to her chest, glancing up from another paper heart and feigning offense. "Are you making fun of me?"

Chuckling, I hold up one of the cards and wave it around. "You know, these things could be said about me just as easily."

“Happy Old Maid's Day?” Alecia says, screwing up her face, "Uh-uh. Girl, you can be an Old Maid by yourself, *I* prefer bachelorette; bad b is also acceptable."

I chuckle, joining her on the floor.

“So,” she says, leaning against the back of the couch. "I was serious about you getting back out there. Anyone you're interested in?"

"Ugh, no, thank god." I say, "I'm way too busy." That and the fact that most relationships don't even last that long anyway, what's the use pouring into something that'll just crumble, or someone that will leave you? No thanks.

My sister heaves a sigh of exasperated affection, giving me the 'I'm not disappointed, but I am concerned about you' look I've come to know very well.

My lips curve in a weak smile. I don't want to think about guys right now, and by guys, I mean, Aviel. He's a selfish and arrogant man who runs an illegal business and god knows what else. I shouldn't be attracted to him, let alone waste my time imagining that he could be a decent person. But I keep reliving the passionate, heated encounter we had had. The memory is a hot brand on my mind, undeniable and impossible to ignore...

I try to quell the heat gathering inside me, but it's like trying to douse a wildfire with a glass of water. The feeling of his lips on my skin still burned and refused to fade away – I can't seem to forget what he did to me, even if it made my skin crawl. A shiver runs through me - why did some part of me enjoy it?

Now that I know he isn't human at all, I should be running miles in the opposite direction. But, a strange hunger, a wild impulse, stirs within me – and I still feel the ghosts of the aftershocks of my orgasm. The truth is, I crave more of his touch, despite the terror it brings.

"Adora, what's going on?" Alecia gives me a knowing look, she can always tell when something is off with me.

I shake my head, tucking the secrets of what transpired between Aviel and me tightly away. "Nah, nothing important," I say instead. "It's been a rough few weeks. Just want to make sure we treat ourselves this Valentine's Day."

"Aww, Adora, thanks for everything. I wouldn't trade you for anything—well, maybe a ticket to Disneyland," She laughs.

"Girl, same—but book me a flight to the Bahamas. Okay?" I grin back in kind, then turn to my raggedy zipped duffel bag on the floor, with thick stacks of monetary notes assembled, wrapped in plastic bags, and shoved inside.

Alecia's gaze follows mine, her expression quickly changing, "Is that all of it?" she whispers.

"Most of it," I reply, shrugging my arms through the sleeves of my coat in one fluid motion, "I'm still waiting for the loan at work to be cleared."

I turn back to Alecia propped against the couch, sadness spreading over her features. "I hate to have caused-"

I quickly step forward and pull her into a hug. “Don’t you dare finish that.” I scold her gently before pulling away.

She shakes her head and puts back on a brave face. “Sorry, don’t let me keep you.”

“I’ll be back before you know it, then we can have dinner with non-alcoholic wine, your favorite."

She chuckles and rolled her glistening eyes, dabbing at her eyes with her shirt, “Ugh, kill me.”

“Not until we've had our best Valentine’s Day yet,” I say with a wink. But all too soon, it's time for me to go.

We sacrificed so much, sold everything we could, and borrowed the rest to pay back what I owed. But, seeing my sister recovering is a reminder that it had all been worth it, and I will never regret it.

A bitter gust of wind tugs at my clothes, but the cold air feels good, invigorating. It's mid-afternoon, I have to hurry to make it to the cab that is waiting for me. I wave to Alecia before slamming the door shut, and we're off in a flurry of snow and exhaust fumes.

I sit alone in the backseat of the cab, surrounded by the smell of sharp, cheap cologne and a hint of cigarette smoke. I tap my foot anxiously, constantly refreshing my bank account all through the drive. The funds hadn't been wired yet, and I have an eerie feeling that something isn't right.

With shaking fingers, I shoot a quick message to HR, asking them if there was any problem. A peculiar sense of apprehension begins to spread through me. Something definitely feels wrong.

We arrive at my destination, a grand, old building, but nondescript in that there is no signage, and I step out of the vehicle cautiously.

My heart pounds faster as I approach the entrance. The exterior’s white stone facing gleams in the waning sunlight, and when I peer inside through the tinted windows while walking along the sidewalk, all I can see is an expansive hall with high vaulted ceilings supported by thick, looming pillars, the space furnished with plush velvet seating that comes in an array of colors from deep reds, greens, and blues to lighter pastel tones. I get the distinct air of a gentleman's club when I spot an oak bar at the back of the room. But from here, it appears empty.

Taking a deep breath, I step up to the heavy front door and rap my knuckles against it, and before long, the door opens, the smell of cigars hitting my nose. A figure appears, a scowling doorman, who looks me up and down.

"Adora Coleman?" He says.

I nod quickly in affirmation, "Yes."

"Come on inside." He says, abruptly turning on his heel and beginning to walk towards the interior of the building. I'm ushered past tables, vintage paintings and tapestries to the basement of the building, where a towering, stone-faced man is waiting for me—I can't help but note that this guy is even taller than Aviel. It's evident he's used to intimidating people.

"I assume everything is in order?" He asks, his voice deep and gravelly, gaze dipping to the duffel bag slung over my shoulder.

"Yeah—" I croak quickly, "I mean, twenty thousand is outstanding; I'm just waiting for-"

"That wasn't the deal, Ms. Coleman." he interrupts me, his baritone voice filling the room like the tolling of a death knell. "We kept our end of the deal; now it's your turn."

"It's probably just a small issue," I fumble.

"An issue? I hope not." He says, frowning, a menacing glint in his eye. "What did you think, this was going to be easy street? We do business a certain way around here, and we aren't going to change it because you think you can get something for nothing."

The air rushes out of my chest, but I make sure not to shrink. "Look, there's no issue." I correct myself. "I'm sure they are fixing it now. I just need to make a quick call."

He dips his chin once, and I excused myself to a corner near a bank of elevators while he and several assistants begin counting out the money.

I get the busy signal the first time I ring, but the second time around, I breathe a sigh of relief when someone picks up on the other end.

"Thank you for calling Lewis & Co. Environmental Consulting & Development. This is Marissa speaking; how may I assist you?" The voice on the other end speaks, breathing static onto the line.

"Hi, this is Adora," I say quickly, trying to speak with a hushed tone—the tall man's eyes catch mine, and I turn from him.

Mind your own goddamned business!

I clear my throat, "I was waiting for a loan to be deposited in my account—I was told it would be today at the latest?"

"I understand that you're calling about the workplace loan program. May I have your name and employee ID number please, for verification purposes?"

"Yes. It's Adora Coleman, my employee number is 234124."

"Thank you Ms. Coleman, I'd be happy to help you with that. Give me a moment while I pull up your file," I hear keyboard chatter in the background, and my eyes dart back to the men still counting the monetary notes. They are piling up and arranging stacks of bills in order of different denominations, counting them, and feeding them into a money counter that sits atop the desk, the chatter filling the room. "I believe I recall this loan being processed, it was supposed to be dispersed to your account."

My pulse quickens as relief rushes through my body, "I was worried, I mean—I didn't see it come in."

But there's no response from Marissa on the other end, and the more seconds that pass by, the more the knot in my stomach tightens.

"Ms. Coleman—"

"Yes?" I whisper, like a prayer.

A mouse clicks, and Marissa's voice soon follows, seeming to come from far away while she continues to type, "Ms. Coleman, it appears our lender has decided to delay the transfer."

My stomach drops to my feet after hearing words that sound so innocuous yet so dangerous at the same time, "A delay?" I choke out.

"I'm certain it's nothing serious," she says reassuringly. Still, it doesn't sound convincing either way, with all these witnesses around me silently judging that my debt repayment seems on tenuous ground.

"It's likely some information just needs to be re-confirmed. May I transfer you over to FlexFunds Paycheck Lending's administrators? There might have been a typo or something in the application."

"That's fine, I authorize you to transfer me to their administrators," I speak with a confident air, but my self-assurance barely masks my dread as doubt starts to gnaw at the edges of my mind—I'd *been* approved; I know I had. It should be as simple as going through the protocol of it all.

"Please hold," Marissa instructs, her voice already fading as the line clicks.

I wait several long moments more, the men have stopped counting and now look at me, waiting for my phone call to end, my silence only increasing their scrutiny.

Finally, I'm connected to the Credit and Underwriting Department of FlexFunds.

"Thank you for holding," the terse and nasally voice on the other end responds. "How can I assist you?"

Forcing myself to concentrate, I recite the details of my loan application. The call goes on and on, with more questions and answers than I can keep track of. I feel like I am going in circles, but I keep at it until finally, the status of my application becomes clear:

"Denied."

The news is like a sledgehammer against my chest. My mind takes off in a dozen different directions, too fast for me to think. I swallow hard and try not to panic, trying to focus on one thing and one thing alone: finding a way to fix this error.

“De-” My eyes flicker to the waiting men, watching me intently, their eyes piercing right through me, just as I catch myself from saying the word aloud. I must not break character. “Do you know how?” I ask as calmly as I can manage through my shock.

“After a thorough reevaluation and review of your application and credit history, we have determined that your credit score does not meet our minimum requirements for loan approval—”

The woman continues to drone on with her canned response, her words fall on deaf ears as I struggle to process what the hell is happening. “We encourage you to take steps to improve your credit and reapply in the future...”

The rest of the words recede into the back of my mind as my thoughts scream. I can feel the panic rising within me, but I have to stay composed, “Wait, we talked about this already. I met the requirements—”

I’m only met with a useless recommendation that if I suspect there are inaccuracies in my credit report, they can assist me to file a dispute with the credit bureau—but, of course, I don’t have time for an entire investigation into the matter, because I only have until midnight to meet my deadline.

I needed the money now.

Wordlessly, I end the call. My whole body feels paralyzed—I have no way of getting out of this mess. Fifty percent interest? That's an extra hundred thousand dollars that I don't have!

My head spins, and my legs nearly give way as I return to the tall man and try once again to reason with him.

"Please, just give me until tomorrow to sort all of this out," I beg.

"Of course," he says, crossing his arms across his broad chest, "Tomorrow with fifty percent interest on the balance."

"But I can't afford another fifty percent!" I could hardly even afford to put food on the table. The only other person I could think of was Aviel — a last resort of desperation. "Please, Aviel can sort all of this out once I get a hold of him!"

The tall man's eyebrows rise, and he almost looks like he pities me, "I'm sure he can. You have until midnight before we charge the additional interest—call him soon."

Tears threaten to spill, but I blink them away. I would survive this ordeal.

"Fine," I say with a determination that surprises even me, "I still have until midnight, right?" I ask.

"Of course."

With a feeling of dread and desperation, I flee the building. It's as if I'm starting all over again, and I hate that the only person I can think of to call right now is the last person I want to see.

I quickly dial Aviel's assistant, John, cursing myself for never asking for Aviel's personal number when I had the chance. When John answers, my hopes are dashed once again; Aviel isn't home, and John isn't sure when I could get a hold of him. Not only that, but a funds transfer of twenty thousand would require authorization that wouldn't take effect before midnight. There was nothing John could do besides try to call whoever he could and make inquiries.

When I beg, he gives me Aviel's personal contact—my last hope. With trembling fingers, I dial, praying for a miracle—but a cold automated voice invites me to leave a message instead.

So, I do.

I leave a tearful message for Aviel to call me back, then wearily make my way back home to be with my sister on the worst Valentine's Day yet.

I settle further into my bath, sinking deep into the embrace of the tub's warm water, closing my eyes. Surrounded by gleaming marble tiles and the sweet aroma of lavender, I envision my plan coming to fruition. My whole body tingles with anticipation, I let it build for a few glorious moments before I release it in a slow, steady breath.

A few moments pass in silence until Jordan enters the room with my phone. On cue, it vibrates.

"Let it ring," I say, my voice low and steady.

Joe stands there, looking at me apprehensively as it vibrates again, "Turn on the voicemail," I command.

He opens up my voicemail messages and places the phone at the edge of the tub, and a ripple of excitement rushes through me.

For a few moments, there's only silence, until it's interrupted only by the faint crackle of static, followed by shallow, uneven breaths —Adora's breaths. The anticipation mounts when finally, it comes—the sound of her voice, broken, hiccuping, and trembling as she begs for help, meets my ears as if she were right here beside me.

"A-Aviel? It's Adora—I know I probably shouldn't be bothering you with this...You were the only person I could think of..." Adora continues, breath drawn out in a painful staccato as she struggles to keep herself together. Her broken exhales evoke a perverse pleasure inside me.

Her despairing words assail my senses like a hurricane, overwhelming me and sending me into a wonderful chaos within. I sink deeper into the water, savoring the pained sweetness of her neediness and feeling her agony as my own.

"C-can you just...can you get back to me as-as soon as you get this—please?" She chokes on a sob, and her voice trails off.

As the recording ends, I remain motionless, letting the quiet consume me. This experience was even more fantastic than I had anticipated, and an unfamiliar sensation stirs in my depths...something darker than before, as I come to realize that this isn't enough.

There is something else lingering in my soul, something forbidden yet irresistible. Her pure emotions have become a dangerous addiction and induce a pull that I find impossible to ignore. They resonate deeply with me in a way I've never experienced before, igniting a temptation I am determined to quench. I'm in uncharted waters here—no human has ever triggered such a visceral response within me prior.

For a moment, I am lost in thought, remembering how she told me to leave and slammed the door in my face with such force that I was certain she had shattered something inside me. This moment has all but made up for that.

“Sir?—" I would have stayed there forever if I didn’t hear a soft voice cut through the silence. “Sir, will you call her back?”

Regardless, the recollection gives me a newfound vigor, and as I look at Jean with a knowing smile, I speak with words that seem to echo across the room. “No, I’d hate to intrude on Adora and her sister on their beloved holiday; let them enjoy the remainder of their *"Happy Single Losers' Day"* without interruption.” I chuckle softly and utter.

"Tell me, what do you think of me getting into property development in earnest?"

My assistant blinks, "Property development, sir?"

My lips curve into a sneer as I answer, "I think I've begun to develop a certain passion for it."

He seems hesitant to respond, observing me carefully before muttering, "But you already have a business that takes up quite a bit of your schedule." Dully, my aide continues, "In fact, lately, you've been a bit...preoccupied."

I feel my upper lip lift in a snarl, "You know what? I think it would be a good idea for you to take the rest of the day off."

Jacques lingers as though he expects further explanation from me, and he looks like he's about to protest when I hold up my hand and say, "With pay. I'm in a good mood today, so get out of my sight."

"Well then, sir, *Happy Single Losers' Day* to you," Jed says.

The not-so-subtle shade wears away my enthusiasm, and my smile slides off my face. "What did you say?" I dare him to repeat it.

"*Happy Single Loser's Day* to you, sir," he actually has the gall to say again, despite his face growing pallid and his stance rigid.

I narrow my eyes back at him, and my gaze hardens like ice while I look him up and down. I've never felt like carving someone up so much in years. I can see the fear radiating off him, he smells of it, I can almost taste it; yet he does not move from where he is standing. I half respect him for it—I suppose that's why he's been my assistant for so long. But as the lavender oil diffusers fill the air with their sweet scent, it occurs to me that he's not worth leaving this relaxing bath for.

He likely figured the same, the sly bastard.

I let it slide, just this once, "Hm, well, savor it."

He nods curtly and turns away from me, retreating into the hallway and leaving me alone with my thoughts.

Justin had been wrong about one thing, though. A preoccupation? Certainly not. I was simply giving Adora the attention due one who sought to challenge me. I know that soon, I will have my reward—the moment when Adora gives in to me.

I spend the following morning pacing nervously in the kitchen, my hands shaking as I prepare tea for Alecia and myself. Distractedly, I set Alecia's tea before her at the table, and she says something in return that my mind barely registers.

My eyes keep flickering to the screen of my phone, desperately seeking a call or notification from Aviel, or even a message from his assistant, my heart beating in my chest.

No calls.

No messages.

Nothing.

Well, nothing besides an alarming message I received early this morning that I dare not read again.

I hastily grab my cup of tea, my eyes darting to the screen of my phone one more time. In a moment of clumsiness, I accidentally spill the hot liquid all over my shirt. "Shit!" I hiss, snatching a paper towel and scrubbing at the mess. I've been a wreck since yesterday, and it doesn't help that I've been having the same recurring nightmare.

"You okay?" Alecia asks, pulling a chair out beside her and holding it for me, "Sit; if you don’t stop moving, you’ll give me a heart attack."

I jab a finger at her, "Don't you fucking dare."

And she only chuckles softly, and pats the seat beside her.

"I...I'm fine," I say weakly, collapsing into the chair she offers.

Alecia's eyes are fixed intently on me, overflowing with sympathy and understanding. I slump forward against the table and exhale a shuddering breath, my gaze drawn to the floor.

"It's gonna be alright," she whispers. She drapes an arm around my shoulders and squeezes me tight.

"Look, we don't need Aviel, or his money," She fiercely declares. "We'll figure out how to come up with the funds ourselves. We just need to get creative." Her voice is steady despite the impossible task before us. "I've been up all night thinking, and I came up with a few things." She rattles off a string of ideas, from launching a GoFundMe page to applying for grants and even pre-approved credit cards. But as creative as her ideas were, none of them would yield the type of money we needed within a day.

It was just like her to try to dive back into work before she was even recovered, and I feel guilty that she should even be worried about money right now too. She'd been up and about this morning before I even woke up, and I already had to stop her from overworking herself with household chores.

I know she wants to contribute, but she needs to take it easy, and I'm sure the stress isn't doing her recovery any good; the thought sobers me, and all I can do is groan in anguish.

"Sorry, Adora, I'm trying my best here," Alecia sympathizes. "I'll try to call around—"

"No!" I cut her off, feeling the tightness rising in my chest. "It's not your fault—"

Before I can explain, my phone suddenly vibrates, silencing me. I pick it up, and my heart leaps with joy as the familiar voice of Aviel's assistant informs me that Aviel had graciously rearranged his schedule to fit me into a time slot this afternoon—I have an hour before he'll be here to pick me up.

I gasp, joy bubbling up inside me like a fountain. Alecia raises her eyebrows at me, and I can't help but leap up and hug her tightly.

"Gotta get ready!" Is my only explanation before I scramble to find something presentable to wear.

A sharp knock sounds at the door, and there stands John, his face an impenetrable mask as usual. His expression makes me dread the appraisal I'm sure will come. To my surprise, his eyes are almost sympathetic as they scan my exhausted face.

I already know I look a mess - I have red eyes from lack of sleep, and I've barely eaten. My baggy sweater with the geometric pattern, mini skirt, and long flat mod boots are my best attempt at a suitable outfit.

At last, he breaks the silence. "Ms. Coleman, you really have no other options?" he asks, his voice flat but not altogether unkind. "You can't seek assistance from family or friends?"

I shake my head vehemently, feeling my throat tighten painfully as I do so. He already knew the answer; why was he asking again? "I need to see him," I reply firmly.

John breathes out a long sigh. "You don't," he says finally, his shoulders slumping, "But I'll take you to him anyway. You'll have to leave your phone behind." He turns away, looking resigned and almost sad.

Outside, clouds gather in the pale grey sky, blanketing the sun. The cold air whips past as we walk down the street, leaving me feeling chilled to the bone despite my coat and thick sweater.

I draw my coat close to me, looking at John's back as it rises and falls with each long stride he takes, his pace making it hard for me to keep up. At last, we reach his nondescript black Corolla, always conveniently parked to ensure I can't see its license plate.

John swings open the door to the backseat and motions for me to climb inside. Before he closes the door, he pauses.

"If you please." He passes me the familiar black blindfold headband, the same one I had had to wear on my first visit to Aviel's residence. Apparently, clients weren't allowed to see where Aviel lived for security purposes. It figured for his line of work, although it's rather ironic that he didn't want or appreciate unexpected guests.

I hear him circle around to the driver's side, then the engine roars beneath us, and we pull out of the parking lot onto the city streets.

As the noisy city gives way to quiet winding roads, my skin erupts in goosebumps beneath my sweater, and I clutch the sides of my seat in total darkness. The bumpy ride makes my head bob back and forth slightly. Finally, riding on smooth pavement again, we stop after several more minutes of silent driving.

When we finally pull up to Aviel's home, John helps me to step out of the car. His arm in mine, he guides me down the winding path lined with trees; I hear their branches rustling in the chill air. I can't help but feel as though I'm being watched, though I can't see anyone—or anything for that matter.

John leads me up a set of steps, finally allowing me to slide off my blindfold. I'm met with familiar massive french doors flanked by two tall, imposing statues of lions, their stone faces reflecting the afternoon's light.

Opening the door, he reveals the magnificent sight of Aviel's residence, with its towering windows and ornate architecture.

John motions for me to enter.

I am a bit hesitant at first, feeling a chill run up my spine as I cross the threshold once again, and for the second time, I feel a strange sensation in the air, as though something ominous awaits me.

Once inside, I gaze around in awe, reunited with the walls and ceilings adorned with elaborate paintings that I hadn't taken the time to truly appreciate the first time. The furniture and decorations are equally luxurious, the marbled black and white checkered floors gleam from a recent polish, and rich runner carpets sprawl across the floor. Even the air seems to shimmer with a faint hint of opulence.

But it's the music that captivates me the most, hitting me the moment I step foot in Aviel's house. The rich and melodic sound of a piano drifts through the corridors like a ghostly mist emanating from the depths of the place, the notes deep and haunting—a beautiful, bittersweet serenade.

My heart swells with a mixture of fear and hope as I stand transfixed in the grand space. Flashbacks of Aviel's true form race through my mind, but no other course of action lies open for me, so I press forward.

I haven't felt motivated to do anything in weeks except to see just how far I can push Adora's buttons before she snaps under the pressure. Another part of me thinks I should step back and breathe again before I ruin everything I've built. But at this point, I'm simply too far gone, I can't help myself.

Up until this moment, she's remained resilient in the face of my machinations while I remained determined to bring her to her knees.

Again.

But today, one day after Valentine's Day, I'm certain that I will conquer her.

A delicate fire, slowly burning the hickory logs, crackles, and spits in the large fireplace set into the wall, warming the room with an orange glow. I sit on the polished piano bench, behind a Steinway grand piano in the center of the living room, beneath airy high ceilings, my fingers tracing out a soft tune. The melodies are both familiar and new, notes of my own creation.

"Sir, Ms. Coleman is here to see you," Jim's voice breaks through the music. He had come to present Adora before me, as I instructed him to — though he hadn't needed to announce her arrival, her scent alone had already alerted me to her presence as soon as she stepped foot in my house.

"Is she?" I temper my urge to look at her, and my gaze does not leave the piano keys.

I sense Adora's confusion at not being greeted; the air is filled with her anxious breaths. Her footsteps are soft, sounding out as she approaches. It has been far too long since she last graced me with her presence—two agonizing days, to be precise.

And now, her petite frame stands just a few short feet away. My flesh tingles as a new wave of nervous energy flows from her body into the air around us, just as her perfume wafts towards me in an invisible cloud of musk and lilac, wrapping itself around me and teasing me with glimpses of what she hid beneath her clothes. If I had a heart, maybe it would beat erratically with excitement.

I keep to my song, my fingers dance with ease over ebony and ivory keys, traversing across the piano in a blur of swift but graceful movements. I press my foot against the sustain pedal and let out a single musical note that echoes throughout the room as if beckoning her to me.

"Aviel..." she says, slightly closer now.

I close my eyes, imagining taking her and spreading her wide for me against the piano.

"I need to speak with you." Adora's voice is somehow both defiant and resigned, delicate and fearless all at the same time—though not so desperate as it had been just the day before.

Pity.

Just hearing her voice ignites a primal hunger in me. I feel my body hum with the memory of her shouting my name in ecstasy. A great move on my part, even though her last move had put *me* in check. Every bit of myself longs to go to her, pull her close to me, and reclaim the realm we had stumbled upon days ago. Instead, I choke back the urge to show how badly I want her.

I take a deep breath; it is time to act like a proper man again, with reason, with restraint, with patience...

A difficult task when all I can think about is how I want to see the look on her face when I erase all the pain with pleasure.

Aviel says nothing, he only dips his head slightly as I speak, his forelocks slipping forward a little—his acknowledgment almost entirely dismissive.

I slide my gaze over him, from the mosaic of tattoos that cover his broad shoulders and defined arms, chest, and torso to the soft leather pants against his long legs. His skin glints in the firelight, and I find myself wanting to reach out and trace the patterns of ink with a fingertip.

A few days ago, he'd taken it upon himself to smooth slide through my apartment and then burglar what he wanted—and now, here I am with my bruised pride, ready to lay all out on the table, and he is all but ignoring me.

Aviel and I remain locked in this tense stand-off, him as still and intimidating as a menacing shadow, me standing before him with my heart racing and fists clenched.

"I must confess," He begins huskily, finally breaking the silence. "I never thought I would see you again..." he traces a pattern on the piano keys, and I listen carefully to their song as it rises and falls, trying to gauge what he's feeling. "And yet, here you are."

"And yet you won't even look at me," I whisper back, but he remains unbothered and continues to run his fingers along the keys.

"You have yet to explain why you are here," he says without missing a beat.

I smooth my clammy palms over my sweater, unable to put into words what brought me back to him; he continues to play, allowing himself to take pleasure in every moment of my discomfort. I know he's waiting for me to grovel; he's just drawing it out.

"You seem to always go out of your way to insult me just when I think I am beginning to understand you," I finally say.

Aviel halts mid-note and looks at me for the first time that day. His piercing eyes bore into me, I sense him taming his words as he replies, "You mistake my frankness for insults, I'm afraid. And I simply don't have the time to coddle you. That's what you want? Coddling?"

I take a deep breath and release it, "I'm not here to argue with you."

"A shame," He says, returning to the keys, "I rather enjoy your attempts to outwit me." He snidely adds, trailing off with a chuckle.

My emotions peak, and I can't hold myself back, "Can you stop being an asshole for just one second?" I splutter, foiling my attempt at composure. "I need your help."

He cuts his gaze toward me, and his playing stops. "Why? Your sister need a kidney again?" He bares his teeth in a wicked grin with a crinkle of his nose.

I'm torn between responding to that and telling him why I am here, and he's lucky my love for my sister wins out.

"I couldn't make the full payment yesterday," I admit with reluctance. I begin to pace around the room. "And the money I was supposed to get to cover my loan didn't come in time to avoid the interest. I tried calling you yesterday, but..."

My throat closes up, and no more words come out. Anxiety consumes me as I continue pacing the room, words pouring out before I can properly assemble them in my mind: "...I can't pay back the loan with an additional fifty percent—I already know I'm going to be late on my rent...."

Gone are all the courage and bravery I had mustered before. Now all that is left is a trembling mess of a girl before him. When I stop before the piano and face Aviel, he stares at me with a mix of disappointment and aggravation.

"You knew the terms of the contract, Adora," he scolds me crisply, cold, and matter-of-fact. "You were told your requirements on your end in good faith that you would meet them. I don't see what I am supposed to do here."

My breath hitches; I know he's disappointed with me, but he has no clue how bad things really are. My chest tight with helplessness, I try to make him understand, "It wasn't my fault! I didn't know my credit agency would misreport my score!" I say, hoping to cut through his icy exterior with the truth. "Right before the transfer!"

His midnight eyes latch onto mine with such intensity that a flush of shame creeps across my cheeks. His lips part, poised to speak, but I beat him to the punch, my words rushing out of me like a cascading waterfall: "I can get the money soon! I need more time to pay it off without the interest! I promise to pay everything back as soon as I get the money—Please!"

"These people don’t work with promises," Aviel begins, and my mind reels because he isn't helping me at all.

"But—" I start to plead, but he cuts my appeal off at the head.

"It is a business," he reminds me silkily, "And it operates as such—"

His words cut short as I interrupt him, spilling out the nightmare that has become my life. "They left a message on my phone!"

Aviel's brows rise up ever so slightly, whether out of pity or sheer curiosity, for now, I have his attention.

I explain how Aviel's lenders, seeing my deteriorating capability to repay my debt, suddenly switched tactics overnight. Texting from a burner phone number, they left a chilling message for me, calling in the debt within twenty-four hours, or they would be forced to collect my sister's heart as payment.

"They promised to do it if I don't pay them back by sunset tomorrow, Aviel!" I gasp; my plea is broken by sobs I can't seem to control, my stomach twisting into knots. "With interest!—" I hiccup.

Aviel's expression softens, but that's the only clue I get of his next decision. "You will have to pay them then," he says lightly, making that statement almost sound like a joke. And as if to punctuate it further, his hands glide back to the keys, and his music floods the room as if he has already moved on with his life while leaving me to wrestle with my own inner turmoil.

"Are you serious?" I croak incredulously over the tune and watch his jaw tick. "...You're really going to let them—"

"I am not your friend, Adora!" Aviel rounds on me, baring his fangs, his voice echoing through the chamber. I stumble several steps away from him. He doesn't even sound like himself. Even John, at the far end of the room, stiffens and turns his face away.

Aviel remains silent for an eternity before speaking in a low voice laced with danger, "I am not responsible for you or your decision-making, nor am I your knight in shining armor to come in and fix it all so you aren't inconvenienced," he goes on mercilessly, "You said you understood the terms. Shall I fetch the contract to show you *once again* what you yourself signed?"

The stillness in the air is broken only by my frantic breathing and the roaring of my pounding heart; I quietly whisper my agreement.

"No. You aren't my friend or my knight. But, I'm willing...I'm willing to do whatever you want if you help me."

Aviel remains unreadable as he considers my daring proposal. He rises slowly from the piano bench and steps forward, coming to a halt in front of me. "Anything?" he asks.

I swallow and will my knees not to buckle under this new kind of scrutiny. I nod before I can give myself the chance to change my mind on the spot. "Anything." My bottom lip quivers, but the word is firm. My heart pounds at the utter recklessness of what I've just offered him.

Aviel snaps his head up to address John over my shoulder. "Leave us," he orders.

I nervously glance behind me in time to see John's eyes widen in disbelief and meet mine for the briefest moment, clearly thrown by Aviel's command.

He seems almost reluctant to go, like he wants to say something, but the look Aviel gives him then is all he needs to realize that it's time to leave. He complies, no argument tolerated. Clearly, if Aviel wills something to happen, it will. Without another moment of deliberation, John crosses to the double doors and slips outside, closing it softly behind himself, and I hear the lock click into place.

"Take a seat there," Aviel gestures with a languid sweep of his arm. I follow the movement to the dark leather Chesterfield couch, with its spiral arms and deep tufted back. It faces the piano, where Aviel had been previously seated.

My skin flushes with apprehension.

"I won't ask twice," he says, his voice laced with warning.

My feet move of their own accord, taking me towards the couch, and my heart thumps as I ease myself onto its soft cushions. The cool leather against my skin sends a surprising chill through me that leaves me trembling.

Aviel returns to his place on the piano bench, our gazes locking as we sit facing each other. The room is thick with anticipation; I wait for him to speak.

"Strip, now," Aviel purrs out in an almost gentle tone, but his words are laced with a razor blade, lingering in the space between us and becoming more potent by the second.

"W-what?" My eyes widen in their orbits, and heat rushes through me.

Aviel leans forward and ices me with his gaze and repeats the words, slowly this time, his tone dripping with honeyed danger: *"Take. Off. Your. Clothes."*

My muscles tense in response to his provocation. I sit there for what feels like an eternity, fighting the urge to obey, but I'm no match for the heaviness of his gaze, and finally, my hands start to move of their own accord as they unfasten the top button of my woolen coat. I glance up briefly, shooting daggers in his direction with my eyes, sending him a silent message, but clearly, I'm sending the wrong one.

My skin prickles as Aviel makes his move. He stands up and slowly steps closer with measured strides, close enough that he surrounds me with his heady aroma of sweet tobacco and warm spice, and I feel the heat radiating off of him as he towers over me. Before I can look away, he takes a punishing hold of my chin. His intoxicating presence is almost too much to bear, and I find myself leaning in closer, glaring up at him, heat growing in my core.

He tilts my head back slowly, making me look up into the fathomless depths of his gaze, and my breath catches in my throat, his lips only a whisper away. His velvet tone slides into my ears like silk when he speaks, his breath a whisper of warmth against my lips: "You are in no position to argue. You have nothing to leverage. Do as I say, Adora."

A shiver runs through me, bringing back the memory of that night he came to my apartment and took me by storm; something primal within me wants him to overcome me—to take me and pleasure me in ways I never imagined.

But Aviel pulls himself away and returns to the piano bench. There, he levels his heated gaze on me, making the hairs on the back of my neck stand up.

My lids flutter shut, I steady my breathing and finish unbuttoning my coat, slipping it off my shoulders; it drops to the floor with a whispery thud. My sweater and then my skirt soon follow, and after a few moments of hesitation, I grasp the edges of my camisole and, inch by inch, expose my skin to the cool air. I pull it off and let it puddles on the floor with the rest of my clothing.

I can feel his eyes on me as each layer of clothing peels off until I finally sit before him in just a brassiere and panties. I slowly unhook my bra, and my nipples harden beneath my fingertips. With my eyes fixed on his, I let my bra, too, fall to the ground.

Aviel's gaze follows each movement as I slip off my panties. Unbidden heat pulses between my legs as the last piece of clothing separating us vanishes.

His darkening eyes roam freely over every inch of my body, studying me intensely. Finally, his lips curl up into an appreciative smile. "Good," Aviel growls, despite myself, the sound of his carnal satisfaction resonates deep in my veins.

A forbidden pleasure stirs in me, leaving my body coiled with anticipation. On any other day, for any other person, I would never have found myself in this situation. But, Aviel's eyes burn on me with an intensity that makes my head spin, and I can feel my inhibitions melting away like wax, leaving me exposed and naked in a way I had never before experienced. This new sensation is both thrilling and frightening, but I can't deny the arousal it brings. In this moment, I realize that I've never felt so alive.

Aviel's voice is like a spell, deep and mesmerizing. "Make yourself wet," he commands. He peers at me as if he can penetrate my very being with his stare, and starts to play again.

Hesitantly, I raise my hand, wetting a finger before tracing a taut nipple with it, gripping the swell of my breasts. I arch my back as I pleasure myself, my breath coming in short, labored gasps, and it draws his magnet eyes to mine again over the piano, more intense than ever before. I watch as desire flashes in the depths of those eyes and my need redoubles.

My fingers snake a path down my stomach and between my legs, feeling my skin goose-bump as I get closer to my wet depths. Slowly, I begin caressing my sensitive bud, before increasing pressure on it, and I can't withhold a moan at how slick I have already become.

Aviel speaks in that same deep rumble as before, stirring more longing in me, "Ahh...your arousal is perfect..." His words force me to deepen the motion of my finger against myself, desire pooling between my thighs, my breaths becoming more and more labored. "Keep going."

My pulse races as my body helplessly responds to his commands and the rhythm of his music. I obey without resistance, my fingers delving deep into my depths, and I'm lost in the sensuous notes of his playing.

Even Aviel's tattoos are hypnotic, changing and shifting along his flesh, like living shadows dancing across his skin. But it's his gaze that continues to draw me in, like staring into a void where nothing existed, just pure Svengali.

"This is a song about a man cursed with immortality, who desperately sought to end his existence time and time again...sad, isn't it?" Aviel speaks, but his subtle air of sarcasm is not lost on me.

It's hard to concentrate on his words, and I don't see the point of why he's saying this, but I continue to do as I'm told.

"Living forever seemed like a miserable sentence to him, yet there is nothing most humans would want more than to be immortal." The melody swells and rises, building to a crescendo that almost leaves me breathless. "They have no understanding at all of what forever truly means."

His words are meant to be truth, but I can't agree with them. "And you do?" I ask, and one of Aviel's dark eyebrows rises.

He stops playing, his fingers settling lightly on the keys. "Absolutely." He replies, his voice dropping just a few notches lower.

"So how could you know how the human in your song feels? You've never been a man."

"I am more than any man." He smirks his agreement. "It is true, my immortality is a part of me as integral as breathing. I have seen every side of this wretched world and have no regrets for my state of being. But, I have lived through the centuries and seen nothing but different types of human wickedness and corruption throughout all my lives," his low voice lingers in the air between us, his heated stare never leaving mine and my own entranced by him, "I've never cared for humans, and it's no wonder why so many of them end up in the Red Pit with my father. The eternal damnation is their own doing, and mortality seems like nature's way of trying to control that evil..."

"Is that how you think of me too? As something wicked?" My voice is barely a whisper, but it carries over the silence between us.

He takes his time, slowly reflecting, "We all have the capacity for evil." Aviel husks out in a veiled manner.

"Then you must enjoy creating opportunities for it." I retort accusingly, "You keep seeking out these tainted humans."

"I didn't tell you to stop, Adora," he points out slyly.

I bite my lip and do as I'm told, my body alive with an alchemical mix of pleasure and discomfort.

The music starts again as if it had never stopped. It's a slower song, this time finding a new rhythm to his melody that perfectly matches my hand's movements.

A potent mix of desire and disgust for him surges through me. My fingers continue their ardent exploration of myself for him, circling my already throbbing clit, and I shudder under the force of pleasure that blooms there.

"I told you already, I enjoy truth, and when people give it to me. So what is your truth, Adora? It seems like you'd do anything for that sibling of yours...Do you regret saving your sister's life now that you have been reduced to selling your body to pay your debts?"

The words are scalding, and my insides burn from the insult, but I don't flinch—I'd never be ashamed of what I must do for my only family. Instead of giving him my guilt or sorrow, I slide my fingers deeper into my folds and feel the heat rise in my cheeks, relishing in the way Aviel's eyes darken with a desire he can't conceal, and a surge of power rises up in me in response.

"What I regret," I breathe, my voice barely audible as I shift to sit upright with my back straight and chin high. "Is ever wanting to be with you for free."

Aviel's playing stops, and the silence is deafening. He searches my expression for something he can't find, and I savor this moment of power over him.

"You couldn't resist kissing me," I go on. "You were so lost in the moment that you moved beyond tempting me and into just...taking what you wanted."

But I can't help the shiver that goes down my spine as I recall how his mouth had felt against mine, the intensity of the orgasm he gave me, and how he'd driven the heavy length of himself deep into my throat. My body heats up further at the memory, and a slow flush creeps along my cheeks.

"You were upset I kicked you out that night..." I whisper into the space between us, remembering his expression as I slammed the door shut in his face, spurs me on, and deepens the pleasure. "You wanted me," I whisper, perhaps unable to keep the desire from my voice. "And you still do."

He rises from his seat, and, like an impending storm, his footsteps devour the space between us. His presence overwhelms me, a swirling wind of electricity, enveloping my body with raw impulse. My pulse quickens, and I tremble in its embrace, all of this an illicit prelude to something longed for, long denied.

I nearly forget why I came here.

"You wouldn't answer your phone when I called.." I challenge him as I look up to meet him head-on, "Did I scare you off?..." I say, almost laughing at the thought of it, and watch his eyes thin, something hungered and possessive burning behind them. "Did I bruise your ego when I rejected you? Did I break your heart?"

He surprises me, taking my throat in a cold grip, cutting off my breath, and pulling me to him, sending a feverish wave of heat pulsating through my body. His mouth twitches up with amusement in a smile that unnerves me even as it arouses me. He leans closer. "I have no heart to scare off, let alone to break." Aviel's expression is a mix of amusement and menace as he releases me.

I sink back onto the couch cushions and inhale deeply, trying to reestablish my breath, my entire body shaking with a combination of adrenaline and anticipation; his presence over me still felt.

"Make no mistake," he continues, leaning down and scorching a finger down my face. "You did something to me that night. You stirred something within me that I thought long dead."

His piercing gaze is almost unbearable as I stare back with defiance. "What's that?" I breathe out.

My breath hitches in my chest as his body slides between my open legs, sending a wave of weakness through me.

"Desire," he rasps, his voice low and dangerous. "I haven't felt anything like it in decades. And it's all because of you."

He sinks a hand behind my head and pulls me in close, and I let out an unplanned moan as the pressure of his lips crashes down onto mine, my body responding to his touch instantly despite myself.

My heart races as his lips move hungrily against mine. I cling to him, my fingers weaving through his locks, our tongues passionately twining together in a dizzying kiss, lips locked in a fiery embrace.

He pulls me closer, slamming my body against his. Then without warning, I feel the air around us shift, and his movements grow in intensity. He moves his fingers to where mine had once been, slipping past my slick folds, and I stifle a cry as he enters me, my body arching up to meet him.

I moan into his mouth, growing wetter while his thumb circles my sensitive bud, and he pushes me further and further into ecstasy until I'm crying out, giving myself over to the sensation. My fingers dig into the hard planes of his back, and I feel his muscles flex with every movement of his lips and hands.

A chill runs down my spine as I gradually become aware of an otherworldly and scintillating sensation gliding over my skin -- a feeling of movement beyond the touch of Aviel's hands. I open my eyes and gasp when I see his tattoos contorting with a living force. The ink of

Aviel's designs uncoil with a will of their own; the intricate patterns undulate up in all directions, their tendrils molding over my skin.

I clasp a hand against my thigh to stop the tattoo from moving, but it's no use; the lines of ink chase over the skin beneath my palm, intent on claiming every part of me with their enigmatic grace. My body pulses with a strange foreign energy, the inky tendrils searing my skin with an intensely pleasurable heat, twisting and shifting as if my skin were an open book and Aviel's tattoo ink was the story of his desire written on every page.

I watch, spellbound, as he draws closer, his mouth inches away from mine, and I draw sharp breath with equal parts fear and pleasure.

"Are you afraid?"

Heat rises in my cheeks, and I writhe as the sinuous body art tightens around me, gripping me like a vice and dragging me back against the sofa. I'm pinned onto my back, the leather armrest digging into my spine, and I struggle to free myself. I can feel my breath quicken, my heart racing as the relentless hold on me intensifies.

Unable to speak, I nod.

"Good," he murmurs, and the pressure builds up, hotter, tighter, and faster, his fingers moving in and out of my wet depths. "Fear is a powerful thing—it reminds you of the line you mustn't cross."

My pulse thrums in my ears until I can't hear anything else but my own breathless pleasure noises. I press my eyes shut, clenching around him, my body responding hungrily to his touch. His fingers are buried deep inside me, and with every movement of his hand, he hits another sweet spot, kissing and sucking my neck tenderly as he continues his torment.

I bite my lower lip, my hips rocking against his hand. My body tightens until I break under the waves of pleasure until I can't even concentrate enough to breathe.

My head falls back, and I let out a guttural moan while orgasmic sensations pulse through me, and I see white spots in front of my eyes. I lay there for a moment, dazed and euphoric, and I can only gasp for breath, knowing I have just experienced something extraordinary.

Aviel's low whisper breaks the thick cloud surrounding us, "I'll help you with your problem," He pulls his fingers out slowly, torturing me once more, and withdraws his hand and tattoos both from between my legs in a rush of heat. His lips curve into a smile as he straightens up to admire his work, the satisfaction of seeing me come undone fully evident on his face. "Let me show you what I can do."

I wonder what the hell I'm doing, my mind screaming for me to retreat as Aviel pushes the vibrator deep inside me with a force that makes me whimper, but I am powerless against the sensations rippling through me as his tongue flicks over my clit.

His favorite pastime now is making me come until I beg him to stop, while my favorite pastime is letting him. I need to go to work but can't find the willpower to pull away from him.

Aviel increases the pace, making me cry out as the vibrations make the pleasure ten times more intense. I feel myself gripping his bed sheets, helplessly succumbing to his touch. His skillful hands know exactly how to make me writhe in pleasure, and I moan under his ministrations. I can't hold on any longer and reach a shattering climax against his tongue.

"N-no more," I sigh. Definitely, no more, my lady parts scream at me. They need recovery time, and he's pushing me too far.

Aviel only pauses to chuckle darkly, "Don't try to pretend you're not enjoying it."

The vibrations against my inner walls make me moan despite myself, and I have to admit he's right. "But, I'm gonna be late for work if we don't stop this," I gasp, because it's the only thing that will make him let me go.

"Call in sick," He raises his head again, and his smirk is too smug not to give him a shove. I attempt to pull away from him, but all it does is make his grip tighter.

"I can't afford to call in sick," I lament.

Aviel managed to renegotiate with the lenders, prolong the time I had to repay them by two weeks, and cease the interest accrual for that length of time. He talked them down to one-fifth the interest rate I already owed, even covering the payment—an additional twenty grand that I insisted on paying him back, bringing the total of my outstanding debt to forty grand. A far cry from the one hundred grand that I owed just a day before, so I couldn't be more grateful. Of course, all that doesn't include the money borrowed from friends and family, rounding out to an additional ten grand.

Aviel's answer comes darkly, "What you can't afford is me not being satisfied."

He pulls the vibrator out of me, and I go limp on his king-sized bed, completely spent. But his mouth is more serious now as he replaces the vibrator with lips and tongue that explore me for my pleasure. My body jerks against him, involuntarily giving in to his persuasive movements until, finally, my legs give in from sheer sensation.

Despite the icy exterior, he always kisses me tenderly, like he wants to savor the moment. And I have caught him looking at me, his midnight eyes gaze into mine as if they are trying to unravel the mystery of my soul, and he can't quite figure me out.

It's a dangerous game we are playing, of course, but I'm drawn to him like a moth to a flame. I just hope I won't be caught up in a fire I can't escape.

"What's so important at your work that you're in such a rush to be there instead of here with me?" he asks with a droll tone, his hand on my belly sliding up, then squeezing my breast, which makes me squirm.

"I have to—" I moan, "We're supposed to be hearing good news from the investors for the housing development project." I am genuinely excited to hear back from them. Despite my prior lack of sleep, and incredible stress over the past few weeks, I managed to help my team finish our proposals, and we delivered an impressive presentation. "I want to pay you back."

Aviel rolls his eyes. "You can do that here," he murmurs as he settles between my thighs, and I shudder, feeling the heavy length in his pants brush against my folds.

"No, I really can't—" One of his sweet kisses distracts me from my annoyance, and I can't help but melt into him.

I swear Aviel is too damn cocky, but it's not like he doesn't have the right to be. He has a point, it is so much nicer lying naked in his bed than getting dressed and facing the cold wind.

I can't figure out why I'm so attracted to him. Sure, he's undeniably charming and passionate in the bedroom, his kisses are addictive, and his touches make my body sing, but, I need to be realistic. Aviel's *not* my boyfriend. I don't know what we even have together; it's definitely more of an entanglement than a relationship. Even if whatever it is has me reeling with need and desire, it's healthier to cut it loose before things become too serious—or rather, I get too attached. And being beholden to him makes me feel a little bit too vulnerable, which will never work out.

"Aviel," I shake my head, after a few more moments of wrestling with my thoughts, "I can't... I need to head out."

He finally stretches over and kisses my forehead before he gets up—and I nearly moan in protest in spite of myself.

"Make that sound again, and I'll make you stay longer," he promises, holding me there a little longer, his eyes intense with banked heat and his expression turning slightly severe.

"That's a tempting offer," I reply cheekily, "unfortunately, my team needs me at the office."

"Unfortunately indeed," he replies dryly and lets me up to hop off the bed. I can feel his eyes following me into the bathroom, where I freshen up, apply minimal makeup, and straighten up my clothing. Ten minutes later, I'm rushing out of his bedroom, so I won't be late for work.

Aviel surprises me, pulling me back around the waist and slamming me into him before he kisses me with a raw passion that surprises me even more than my previous reactions to him. The long kiss promises another intense session of pleasure. He releases me before slapping my butt and chasing me out the door with a grin. I almost float away, my entire body tingling with pleasure and anticipation—until the cold reality of work beckons.

Seated in the conference room for an emergency meeting, I do my best to put forth a brave face, surrounded by my colleagues, as well as various documents, blueprints, designs, research, and proposals for the project for economical and sustainable housing.

We had all worked tirelessly trying to secure the necessary funding and make this venture a reality. With a significant role in this project, it would be an extraordinary milestone in my career. Most of all, the vital aid it will offer to the deprived families in this city would be invaluable. That's where my heart really is.

Suddenly, the meeting room doors burst open as Thomas, one of the senior team members, shoves his way inside, his face pale and drawn.

"We have an issue," he begins, his voice trembling with anger, "I just got a call from one of our main potential investors...I can't believe this—"

The murmurs around the room fade into an uneasy hush as Thomas struggles to control himself enough to deliver the news. Finally, he states: "*Green Builders* just gave us a call, and they've pulled out."

Fuck.

Tension fills the air, and collective groans of disappointment ensue. I'm in tremendous shock myself; our presentation had gone over well, and was given a warm reception. *Green Builders'* representative had been highly interested. Had we missed the signs?

"Our pitch was on point, right?" I say, trying to keep my composure and remain upbeat; my voice manages not to falter despite my inner turmoil. "Don't we still have two other investors willing to come aboard? "

Thomas shoots me an almost-glare from the corner of his eye. "It's not that easy," He explains with a sigh, his sloped shoulders slumping with the weight of defeat. "This is the second major investor that's pulled out."

Rohit, Winter, and I exchange wide-eye glances.

"The second?" Rohit inquires, aghast, his thick black eyebrows shooting up.

Thomas nodded curtly, his lips pressed into an impenetrable line. "That's right. *Housing for Humanity* has already declined. This morning."

I swallow my dread, "But what about *The Community Renewal Initiative*? We haven't heard back from them yet, right?"

"That would be the case, but word is they're planning to decline too because of a competitor's similar project—" Thomas looks down at the project sheet, marked up with red ink highlighting all the investors' concerns.

My heart sinks. I draw in a sharp breath, my hands curling into fists. I didn't want Thomas to see my own shaken confidence. Of all the things to happen——why now?

Winter leans forward, her cool blue eyes wide with determination. "Can't we just try to pitch our idea to other people? We can't stop right now when we're so close!" I admire Winter's fierceness; she's just as passionate about the project as I am.

"It seems our competitors caught wind of what we were doing and wanted to take advantage of the opportunity," Thomas said. "They're apparently offering a better deal and have already secured a lot of the funding. Our investors don't want to miss out on the opportunity, so they've pulled their resources from us."

My mind races. Who could have approached our investors with a similar project? We've been working on this for months, and I assumed we were ahead of the game. The sheer amount of work put in so far, including demographic research, cost analysis, and construction blueprints, wasn't something we could just throw away. We even managed to work around multiple restrictions. Who had come out of nowhere and undercut us?

"What's the name of the other company?" I ask Thomas.

"*Redevelopment Solutions*," he says, raking his fingers through disheveled brown curls. "They're a company with similar interests in this city."

My thoughts whirr rapidly. I frown, but the name doesn't ring any bell.

"Why haven't we heard of them before?" A pensive Rohit leans back into his chair, frowning.

"Isn't it just perfect?" Thomas's expression turns acidic. "I heard they've only been around for less than a year."

Rohit drums his fingers on the table, deep in thought.

"But we researched other development projects being proposed and contacted the competing developers," I say, my skin beginning to chill at the revelation. "Noone mentioned a *Redevelopment Solutions*."

Thomas gives an apathetic shrug. "Then our research wasn't exhaustive enough, so they managed to blindside us out of nowhere," he remarks, his words filled with bitterness. I shrink in my seat. "They're a subsidiary of *Keystone Builders Inc.*"

I've heard of *Keystone Builders*, a behemoth of a corporation, but I didn't expect they'd be one of our competitors. From its own construction suppliers to its multi-national development projects, *Keystone* had grown to a size that made it a force to be reckoned with. I'd come into contact with *Keystone* before in my university days, but I never thought they'd be the types to chase after little projects like ours. Few would take a chance on a company they'd never heard of against a renowned brand like *Keystone*.

"Even more worrisome is that their main investor is bankrolling a good portion of their project, mitigating their costs for the development stage and risks for the investors. It looks like they have a lot of influence behind them." The growl in Thomas's throat is audible.

"Which investor?" Winter asks, looking like she wants to fight them herself.

"They're anonymous." Thomas folds his arms over his chest.

The project is in jeopardy, and the worst part is I feel solely responsible for not trying hard enough to find out what companies we were up against. I wish I'd done more.

"Unbelievable," Winter curses, her face turning a shade of red. "*Green Builders* really let us down."

The murmurs of the meeting slowly quiet down as it becomes evident that our original plans won't be continuing as smoothly as we thought.

"We may have to think about putting this project on pause if we can't compete and start brainstorming new project proposals. Winter, I recall you had some unique ideas." Thomas soon dismisses us all.

I'm filled with regret; if this project is my baby, it feels like I might be forced to abandon it when it needs me most.

I sit in my cubicle, gnawing on my thumbnail at my desk as I turn over every possibility in my mind. I'm desperate to come up with a solution, one that will make up for my earlier mistake of not finding out about *Redevelopment Solutions* sooner. I know very little about them, but I'm determined to learn more. I call around, trying to gather any intel I can, but I'm met with dead ends. But it's useless; no one seems to have heard much of them.

My thoughts drift back to everything that led to this situation. I thought I had done everything by the book; I'd done my due diligence, followed all the necessary steps, and yet, I had missed something crucial and failed miserably.

It's become routine for me to visit Aviel in the mornings or evenings a few times a week, and though I'm usually excited to hear from him, I can't bring myself to answer the phone when he calls. All I can manage is a sigh because, with everything that's happened today, I'm just not in the mood.

I twist the key to the door of my apartment, pushing my way inside and stumbling over the threshold, my head pounding and my heart heavy. My day has been a complete disaster, and its disappointments leave me emotionally exhausted. The housing project I've been pouring my heart and soul into has all but fallen apart, and now I just want to curl up in bed and forget about the world, but when I open the door, I'm not alone.

"Adora! Look who's here!" Alecia's voice resounds from the kitchen, startling me out of my thoughts.

There, seated at the table with a glass of wine in hand, is Aviel. Dinner is on the table, take-out that he must have ordered in. The array of colors and textures spread across the table, and the sumptuous smells take me away from the reality of my problems; steaming noodles, freshly grilled vegetables, and bright red curries. The aromatic scent of spices wafts through the room.

There's a flutter in my chest at the sight of Aviel himself, but then I feel myself sink into misery again. Alecia’s concerned gaze implies she knows something's wrong; "Adora?—" she starts, but I cut her off.

"What is he doing here?" My voice quivers as my gaze meets Aviel’s across the room, and I bend down to hastily unlace my boots.

Quick to rise from his seat, Aviel crosses the room in swift strides, just as I stand up again. "Waiting for you," he says smoothly, taking my jacket and bag from me and hanging them up.

Turning back to me, he reaches out, pushing my chin up, attempting to look into my eyes, but I close them.

"Adora." he breathes out, his voice a mere whisper.

I lower my head, not knowing what to say. His closeness causes me to shiver involuntarily; I can't ignore my body's reaction to his voice and the proximity to him. But I don't want to feel this way. Not now that everything has fallen apart.

He leans in closer to whisper next to my ear, his breath fanning my skin. "Tell me what's wrong."

His words trigger something, they unravel a knot within me that makes the tears pour uncontrollably out of my eyes, and end up sobbing on his shoulder.

"Everything!" I wail, my voice muffled in the silk of his shirt, and hot tears spill over my cheeks. "The housing development project basically fell through; the investors are all dropping out. I don't know what to do." My words tumble out in a rush, hitching over my sobs and shaky breaths. "And, I still owe twenty grand in two weeks." I laugh bitterly, and even though, with the help of Aviel, I'd managed to temporarily escape the inevitable, and I don't know if the investigation into my misreported credit score will be resolved within the time I have left.

With every word I utter, his arms wrap tighter around me until, eventually, my crying ceases, and exhaustion sets in. He removes a handkerchief from his shirt's breast pocket, gently dabbing away the tears from my cheeks and the corner of my eyes. "Don't be silly," he says softly.

"We'll just have to figure something out before you run out of time." He speaks as if it were just another objective and not a life-threatening crisis. A part of me can appreciate that.

Alecia gazes at us from her seat with a look that I find too eager. "See, Adora? You're not alone. You have me," She says, but her smile becomes mischievous, "And apparently Aviel..."

I can see the pointed look of warning Aviel gives her at her remark, even if there's no real heat in it, and she simply smiles back at him, thrilled. Then he turns to me and draws me in close, his lips softly pressing against my hairline. My cheeks flush with warmth; he was never this affectionate with me in public—yet here we are. I let him guide me to the table with a gentle hand on my lower back.

His warmth lingers as I take a seat beside him. With a questioning look at the table, I take in the extravagance of the food from Koi Thai, one of the city's most luxe Thai-Japanese fusion restaurants.

Gathering what shreds of dignity remain, I wipe away the tears with my sleeve and breathe shakily. "What's the occasion?" I ask, pulling a glossy black paper box closer.

Aviel slides into the chair next to mine and pushes a wine glass across the table with a wry smile. "This was meant to be a celebratory one - we were supposed to toast to your good news...but it seems this wine can't quite bring the desired vibrancy." He fastens his gaze on mine, dark eyes flickering with a hint of mischief, and I feel myself melting away in its depths. "Interesting choice, I might add."

And by 'interesting', I know he means 'cheap and horrible'.

"Shut up, Aviel." I say, nudging him in return, and even he can't hide the small smile that tugs at his lips.

"See? I told you!" Alecia chimes in triumphantly, her voice full of knowing and her glass likewise filled with de-alcoholized wine. "This stuff is depressing."

“Whose fault is that?" I return with an extravagant scoff. "We can't do shots tonight either, thanks to you."

"She has a point." Aviel observes with soft laughter.

"Fine. Point taken." Alecia tilts her glass back and takes a hearty gulp.

"Mourning bad news calls for the appropriate drink." Aviel concludes drolly, raising his own, "I find this glass of sadness fitting for the somber mood."

We laugh at the absurdity of it all, a little bit of cheer coming back into my mood, "Well, that doesn't explain all this good food." The steam billows up from bowls brimming with aromatic sauces as I test the noodles with my chopsticks, "Don’t you think cold pizza would’ve been a better choice?"

"I know you're not complaining about good food," Alecia says, picking up a taro and bamboo shoot spring roll. "I'm hungry as hell, so if you don't want yours, we'll eat it for you."

Aviel advises me, "Listen to your sister." His voice drops as he edges towards me on his seat, a certain glint flaring in his eyes. "Besides, there's always time for something good to eat."

Heat flares in my cheeks, and I can't help it — the moment he looks at me like that, my body wants to melt for him.

"Um, y'all need a room?" Alecia interjects with a sly grin pointing her chopsticks at us. I roll my eyes and would have kicked her under the table if she hadn't just had surgery.

Perhaps, just for now, It seemed that bad news wasn't so bad after all. Despite everything, I find myself slowly warming to this strange new atmosphere. Why can I see myself getting used to this?

By the end of dinner, we nurse our freshly-brewed espresso drinks, along with our *Kanom Buang*, crepe-like pancakes filled with cream and topped with shredded coconut. Aviel had graciously, if not a tad smugly, brought a bag of luxe Blue Mountain coffee beans.

"To make amends for the awful swill I served you before..." He'd tacked on, when he caught my perplexed expression. "Extra dark roast and sweetened with cocoa liquor."

"What about me?" Alecia pipes up. Aviel only sets a cup of unsweetened strong scented tea on the table before her.

"That new heart was expensive," he counters swiftly. "Drink your bitter herbs."

"Are you serious right now?" Alecia pouts indignantly.

I raise my steaming cup of coffee to my lips, and I can't help but smile around the rim of my mug, admiring the way Aviel is looking out for her health as I am.

As night sets in, we soon find ourselves locked in comfortable conversation. Aviel had left his assistant behind and taken the rest of the day off to visit. Alecia told Aviel some of my most embarrassing childhood moments growing up, which I feebly defended, and Aviel found my youth far more interesting than I did.

We soon find ourselves thrust into a game of two truths and a lie as Aviel regales us with entertaining stories. Some make us laugh uproariously, others chilling our bones with horror, apparently he had some really interesting 'friends of friends'—though he never does reveal which story is the falsehood.

It's a relief not worrying about my own troubles for a while.

Soon enough, Alecia's fatigue sets in, her eyelids drooping with exhaustion. "Besides," she says, "I'm tired of playing third wheel anyway." Her words leave me flushed and flustered as she swiftly raps her knuckles against the tabletop twice and retires for the evening with a parting, "Y'all be good."

Only Aviel and I remain in the kitchen, and I bite at a thumbnail, not quite ready to see him to go yet, even though I know I shouldn't be playing house with him or acting like we have anything serious between us. I never declared we were anything, and he was the same—but the words escape my lips anyway:

"You leaving too?" I ask him, breaking the silence.

Aviel pauses for a few beats, his gaze lingering on mine before he shrugs, "I was thinking about it." he murmurs.

"You could think about staying." I reply softly, wishing he would — and as if he could hear my thoughts Aviel's hand reaches for my chin and tugs it, lightly pulling me in for a kiss, leaving me breathless and I savor the feeling.

"I remember saying the same thing to you," Aviel says against my mouth, his lips curving into a shadow of a smile.

"True," I concede when I finally break away, "But you're still welcome to stay..."

Aviel caresses his mug of coffee with his thumb as he holds my gaze steadily for a few moments longer before letting out a deep sigh. "Normally I'd have taken my leave at this point..."

"But?" I continue for him.

Aviel's gaze alights upon mine, darkening as he spots the challenge in my eyes. My heart stutters at that look, and I find myself holding my breath to see what he'll say next.

"I suppose I can stay," he relents. "Just until you fall asleep."

Somehow I find myself curled up beneath my blankets, but my foggy mind fails to recall how I got here. I nestle into Aviel; my cheek against the warmth his chest and I listen to rhythm of his breathing; each inhale and exhale a tether, a lifeline to this moment. Desperately, I strain my ears to hear the beating of something—anything—but I'm met with nothing but utter stillness.

"I told you, I don't have one." Aviel's words echo in the quiet of the room.

Could such a man feel?...Or love? Strange thoughts pass through my mind as I drift in and out of sleep, my mind too groggy to make sense of them. I feel him looking at me, but I don't meet his gaze, although I can no longer remember why.

My consciousness slowly fades away as he brings my body closer, encircling his arms around me, fitting my head snugly beneath his chin, and engulfing me in his heat and scent. Comfortable in his arms, I feel safe, secure.

I'm suddenly jarred awake by the sharp series of buzzes of my phone. My eyes snap open, and I squint at the light seeping through my curtains. The bed next to me is cold and empty. I fumble for my phone on the nightstand, my vision adjusting to the brightness of my room.

Aviel sent a text saying he'd be busy but to have a good day. It's already off to a good start; I have the weekend off, and Alecia is already up and brimming with energy when I emerge from my bedroom. I have a big day ahead of me, I feel inspired to conduct more research for a project I'm not yet ready to let go of.

Helen and Tayo drop by for a visit, and I fill them in life updates and who Aviel is, since he'd caught Helen's attention leaving in the wee hours of the morning in a luxury Sedan.

"And you had *Koi Thai*?" Tayo asks. "I'm just saying, y'all could've come through with the invite."

Alecia pats Tayo's hand in mock sympathy, "It really did slap though." She laughs before promising to send them home with some leftovers from the fridge—it was too much for us anyway.

Helen, however, ever the overbearing friend, is far more curious about who Aviel is and why he was at the house.

I sigh, "He's...an acquaintance..." I try to dance around the issue, but my friends can see right through me.

"And?" Helen probes shrewdly, sensing I'm holding back.

I exhale, leaning back against the sofa. "He's...strange...in a good way." My cheeks heat up as I murmur, not giving too much away or seeming too thirsty. Our relationship was impossible to label in black or white anyhow. "We kinda have a vibe..."

"Just a vibe?..." Helen says, leaning in, her gaze intense with curiousity.

Alecia is done playing nice and jumps in, blurting out what I can't get around to saying, "The man is fine and has a thing for Adora—"

"Alecia!" I hiss in an attempt to rein her in.

Undeterred, she proceeds to put me on blast, "And Adora likes him too. They've been seeing each other for weeks—"

I'm in a panic now and start to backpedal, "Alecia—"

She cuts me short with a wave, "Girl, bye, I knew it from the first time you went from cursing Aviel's name to cheesing anytime you mentioned him." Alecia rolls her eyes with a scoff. "First of all, you are not slick, second, your big sister knows everything and third, I was diagnosed with a heart condition, not blindness. Yes, you are that obvious, but don't worry, y'all are cute together."

With the end of Alecia's tirade, my friends and family alike share a laugh at my expense. I groan, grab the collar of my sweater and bury my face in it. This is one of the disadvantages of constantly being surrounded by those closest to you; they always have dirt on you.

Finally, we're able to move on from mine and Aviel's situationship. But I keep my nose buried in my shirt; I'm not sure why, but it still smells like him—that subtle blend of luxury cologne and masculine musk that produced an instant warmth deep inside me, the kind you can only feel when your emotions overwhelm all senses.

I stay busy the rest of the afternoon researching *Redevelopment Solutions*—and when nothing comes up, due to their lack of history, I look into Keystone Builders instead. The deeper I dig, the more curious I become. Simon Rogers, the former president of *Keystone Builders*, had been replaced out of the blue by Dustin McCloud just a few short weeks ago.

It looks like someone's gone to great lengths to scrub any dirt on the company; there's hardly anything left for me to find.

I sit at my computer, navigating the tenant websites for several of Keystone Builder's properties—thanks to Tayo getting me in. It's not exactly ethical, but *Keystone* isn't playing fair, at this point, I don't think I need to be held to higher standards.

I squint at the screen, scrolling through the comments. One by one, complaints pile up against several of Keystone's developments. Tales of using legal loopholes to circumvent environmental regulations, neglecting safety and health standards—I smile, perhaps just having found what I needed to persuade the investors to shift their loyalty to Lewis & Co, or at the very least away from *Keystone* and as a result, *Redevelopment Solutions*.

And when I think my day can't get any better, I get a call from the credit bureau, the investigation having proven that my credit is in good standing. Apparently, the error had been caused by a glitch in the system, and henceforth my score has been bumped back up to a 725—much lower than before for all of the money borrowed, but still enough to qualify me for the company loan.

I sink back into the soft cushions of the sofa—exhausted but filled with a contentment and relief that I haven't felt in a long while. I grab my phone to message Aviel:

"Hey! I think I just figured everything out!"

I wait anxiously for his reply. His response comes through with a notification sound that sends a shiver down my spine. A simple "That's great." is all it says, but it sends my heart into a flutter.

"No, really great!" I type back, my grin stretching from ear to ear. I re-read the text several more times before putting my phone down. Things are finally looking up, and my life seems to finally be filled with something other than stress and worry.

The office hums with anticipation as our team plots new tactics in the wake of our fierce new competition. It would be the deciding factor on whether we continue this uphill battle or put the project on ice indefinitely. I sit across from Thomas in the conference room; my eyes focused intently on the project board in front of us with fresh determination.

"I like that," Thomas remarks after hearing a few ideas on outdoing *Redevelopment Solutions*. "But I'm not sure it will be enough. They seem to be offering something extra that we aren't."

My lips remain sealed, but my body leans forward.

Winter pipes in, "What do you mean? They're offering something extra?"

"We've scoured their proposal; they didn't have anything we aren't offering," says Rohit.

"If they have any integrity at all, the investors will go with us," I say confidently, revealing printed sheets of complaints gathered from Keystone's tenant websites. "Keystone greenwashes—they blatantly lie to make the materials they use appear more environmentally friendly than they actually are. Not only that, but they cut corners too. Not only do tenants deserve an affordable place to live, but it needs to be safe and sustainable above all. We can leverage our green building materials and energy-efficient systems, and dedication to safety to set ourselves apart and prove that we care about the environment and the well-being of our tenants."

Thomas steps forward and picks up the stack of sheets from the table, his eyes intently examining the document of my findings. "Adora, where did you—?"

"My sources," I reply coolly, barely letting him finish the question. "Look, I know we can't use these complaints directly, but if an investigation is opened and an inspection done of those properties, it might be enough to sway some of the investors who were considering Lewis & Co. And if this gets public..."

Rohit circles around to peer over Thomas's shoulder, then lets out a low whistle of appreciation, "Wow, you're cutthroat, Adora."

Thomas shakes his head slowly, his expression stern. "If I could prove the method you acquired this confidential information, I'd have you taken off this team."

My heart jumps, and my face drops. I try to maintain my composure, insisting on my stance. "These papers have a voice—what's wrong with letting them be heard?"

"I didn't say they shouldn't," Thomas retorts, his voice chillingly even. "I just said it could cost you your job." His words linger in the air like a gust of cold winter air. For a moment, I feel as though I've already been fired—but then a faint smile tugs at the corners of his lips, admiration glinting in his eyes for my commitment to helping others. "Legally, we can't leverage these complaints as evidence. But we can alert the right authorities to see if Keystone's properties are up to code."

Winter shoots me a confident thumb's up from the opposite corner of the room. I breathe a sigh of relief and smile.

Finally, we discuss raising awareness for the project by bringing it to the community—and perhaps catching the eyes of other investors. With enough organic reach, the campaign wouldn't break the bank. Thomas and the team seem on board, mainly because we all don't want our hard work over the past months to go to waste.

It's going to happen after all; our housing development project is going to help so many people. Maybe, we can light the way for some families in need. But before we've had a chance to even finish discussing its possibilities, I'm summoned to my boss's office.

My usually amiable boss, Victoria Knight, stands rigidly at the opposite side of her desk, her back stiff and her eyes focused sternly upon me.

There's an oppressive silence in the room, broken only by the sound of my heart pounding in my chest so loudly that I swear it must be echoing through the room.

I can sense a storm brewing in her gaze.

What now?

"Adora," She begins her voice cutting through the air like a razor blade. "It has come to our attention that you have been involved in some...business, and it's not exactly above board."

My stomach twists into knots of dread as I ask, "What? What do you mean?" And for a moment, I wonder if somehow, she caught wind of my research into Keystone.

"I understand you've had some trouble with your sister."

Questions swirl around me, and confusion clouds my expression as I utter, "My sister?"

"Adora, during your meeting today, several visitors banged on our doors and stormed our offices demanding to know whether we had an Adora Coleman in our employ."

Terror grips my heart tightly, and I feel my world caving in on me. I'm paralyzed by fear, the atmosphere suffocating me, my innermost fears slowly coming to light.

"Visitors, asking for me?" I furrow my brows, trying to put on a brave front, but I don't remember the last time I've been so scared; it feels as though my world is closing in on me. "What did they want?"

"They appeared to be some collection agency; they barged into our building demanding repayment of some unpaid debt your sister had taken. It was clear they thought you were behind it..." She goes on as if trying to explain an inconvenient truth. "I'm not here to ask questions, and it's really none of my business, but those men were extremely threatening: I fear for you and our employees."

"I-I've delayed repaying back a loan, but I assure you, everything is under control. My application for the loan should finally be re-approved now, and I'll be able to—"

"Adora," she interjects sternly, "security had to escort them out, and I was one second away from calling the police. You put me in a very challenging position here, and I can't risk making our investors or employees feel unsafe here."

"But—"

"Whatever it is you are involved in, Adora, I am afraid I can't let you continue coming to work here if our employees can't feel safe. We're going to have to put you on leave."

"Leave?..." I croak, unable to find my voice. "For how long?"

"That's to be determined; for now, it's until further notice."

The words feel like a death sentence.

"But...but...I *need* this job. " A bead of sweat drips down my face, my heart pounding so hard in my chest that it feels like it would break through my ribs. I blink rapidly, my thoughts a swirl of panic.

"While under this leave, you can consider your options—We will still pay full salary until the end of the month."

"What am I supposed to tell my team?" I stand there frozen, numb, trying to process her words.

"I have an assistant who can pick up your work. Francis will be able to fill in wherever you're needed; if anything, we will speak again on your return." My boss glances away before her gaze lands back on me. "Adora...I'm sorry, but for now, you have to go."

She stands up and reaches out her hand over her desk to shake mine, which is ice cold and trembling.

I stumble out of the building, my belongings cradled in my arms. I feel disoriented and crushed; every effort I had made to provide the company with my skills was worthless in an instant. It's like being thrown off my feet with no means to catch myself before colliding with the ground.

I need my job to take care of everyday bills, and I need that loan to clear the rest of my debt. Aviel managed to get them off my back for a little while, but they came back before my grace period was even over.

What can I do now? I won't cry, I tell myself, and I manage to hold on until I walk through my apartment door and my sister lays eyes on mine. That's when the dam breaks.

Alecia rushes to me and takes me into her arms, caressing my back as her soft hum soothes my soul. "There has to be another way," Alecia whispers as she holds onto me. "We'll find it."

I wipe my face with my sleeve and sniffle. "Maybe I'll try crowd-funding like you said"

Alecia is quiet for a while before replying. "What about Aviel? Can't he just give you the money, and then you can owe him instead of those guys?"

I shake my head, unsure if I could ask him for any more help after he's given so much already. Besides, I don't even know what we are to each other. I'm just that woman who keeps asking him for help.

She lays a calming hand on my arm before speaking again, her voice gentle, "I know he cares about you, Adora."

Alecia doesn't know Aviel very well. It's not that black or white with him; it's a mosaic of grays. But I decide I'll ask him tonight regardless because, once again, I have no other options. So, Alecia and I have dinner together and I muster up the courage to call Aviel. He arranges a ride for me to head back to his place.

When John and I reach his doorstep, Aviel's arms are casually crossed in front of him as he stands in the doorway in nothing but a pair of black slacks, unbothered by the frigid weather that embraces us both.

"You know you don't have to come to me in a crisis every time you want affection?" His expression is both challenging and inviting at the same time.

When I fail to smile, he slips his long fingers around mine. "Come on," he urges me softly.

I pull back and look up at him. My stomach fills with butterflies and I bite my lip, wondering why I react this way to him. "Where?"

"Inside."

I take a deep breath and follow along, not knowing where this night may take us.

He takes us along the hall, the warm, heady aroma of his cologne, a dense medley of sweet tobacco and spice, curling around us like a fog as we enter the living room. He slowly extends his arm, motioning for me to sit, and I succumb to the comfort of his presence, while my heart pounds with anticipation.

The dying sun casts a pallid light through the window, illuminating Aviel's dark hair and pale skin. He watches me for a few moments, his expression unreadable until he finally speaks. "Now, what has you looking so upset this time?"

I clench my hands nervously. "Some guys showed up at my job today, demanding that I pay back what I owe. I was supposed to have more time left before it was due. *And* I all but lost my job, plus the only chance I had to repay the last part of the loan—I need a job to be qualified for it. I don't know what they'll do if I don't pay them."

Aviel's expression turns steely, and his eyes narrow dangerously. "Did they hurt you?" His voice is low but full of intensity.

I tense up and shake my head. "I was in a meeting all day, so I'm lucky in that sense. But now I've got to pay them back or who knows what they'll do next?"

Aviel averts his gaze from me. His eyes roam around the room, brushing past mine and then coming back again. "Adora, I wouldn't let them..." But he trails off and never ends up finishing the sentence.

"Please," I stand up quickly, my hand grasping his arm. "I need your help." My eyes burn with tears, shimmering with emotions that I can't hide anymore.

He lowers his head and rests a finger beneath my chin, lifting it gently. "I'll handle it. They had no right to barge in your workplace like that, especially after we had already sorted things out."

"Thank you!" I embrace him, clinging tightly as his hand settles onto my back; for a moment he feels stiff before softening and allowing me to rest my face against the warmth of him. The muscles in his chest and back move as he breathes, and I listen to the stillness within his chest just beneath my ear.

Aviel's muscles tense up, as if he battles with himself whether to continue this embrace or not. "That's enough of your foolishness, silly human," he finally whispers, his hands gently making contact with me before pushing away.

I grin at his words. They're basically a term of endearment by Aviel's standards.

Tilting my head back, I press my lips to his shoulder and kiss him tenderly, his tattoos, creatures, and patterns alike, shift and whirl around as I move my mouth near them. And when I lift my arms to let my hands slide along his chest, they move in a mesmerizing pattern beneath my fingertips, following the sinews of his muscles and undulating like waves in a pool. For the first time, I catch myself wondering why he's so often shirtless when I see him. Not that I mind, but one thing I know about Aviel is that it has to be more than vanity to him.

My gaze lifts, drifting from the lean cut muscles of his exposed torso to the perfect line of his corded neck that led to the angular features of his face, and finally to meet his dark gaze, and I smirk, "You have something against shirts?"

"What?" He chuckles, and the sound fills the air like a warm bass note, drawing me in with its captivating rhythm.

I love it when he laughs—it makes his whole face light up, and it's one of the rare times I can see unexpected emotion in his eyes, the sort that's too candid for even him to veil.

I grin back, "I'm saying, I can count the times I've seen you wearing a shirt on one hand."

His gaze slowly slides from mine to land back on his body art as though just now considering it. "They like to move around," he finally explains in a murmur, tracing his tattoos with a finger.

Of course, I haven't thought something like a shirt could hinder supernatural tattoos that like to move. I always assumed they could just move unhindered beneath the fabric.

I stared at him and waited for more explanation, but he doesn't offer any along with his slight smile.

A question lingers at the back of my mind; I want to know more. "Tell me about them," I ask.

He pauses for a moment before he nods once as if he realizes that no matter what he says, it won't stop me from asking.

We settle into our places on the couch, shoulder to shoulder. Aviel starts his story, his voice like velvet dripping from his lips, as he reveals the secrets of his past, the images of his stories dancing in front of us.

"It was long ago, in a realm seeped in sin, where a Duke of Hell, known to few and feared by all, had dominion. His authority was absolute and his cruelty, unparalleled. He was the warden of lost souls, chosen for the ability to keep them entrapped in an impenetrable prison from which none who entered escaped.

"That Duke," Aviel intones solemnly, "Was my father. He saw the souls in his care as nothing but playthings to be tormented as he pleased. I refused to be a part of his cruel legacy. I rebelled against my father, vowing to one day find a way to free the souls from their endless suffering. My actions infuriated him but still, I persisted, adamant that even these souls deserved to find peace. I succeeded in freeing those souls but, in doing so, I became a prison myself.

The souls were bound to me, and with them, all of the memories of every experience they've had and everything they've done, every desire their hearts have ever had, no matter how innocent or depraved, every atrocity they've ever committed from the moment they took their first breath until the moment they felt death's grip. The burden weighed down on me like an anchor. Each soul I collected brought nothing more than a surge of repulsion.

Each time I harvested a new soul, they proved my father right about the character of human beings - their penalties were justly deserved."

"I thought you said you don't judge," I say.

"I don't." Aviel lifts his chin. "I remove obstacles to a human's true nature, then, when they prove who they are, I collect." He shifts, and I can see the myriad of creatures and symbols upon his body, shifting on his flesh. I feel a chill as I gaze upon them.

"Those don't look human," I say uneasily, repressing a shiver.

"Their souls take the form most suited to them. Take this rat, for instance," He says as he upturns his wrist to reveal the black, red-eyed creature made of ink that quickly scurries to the back of his hand. "This scamming rat here was a scoundrel who robbed Peter to pay Paul so many times he found himself in crippling debt, all to keep up with his hazardous gambling habit and impress the women who threw themselves at him.

Luckily, he met me. I was gracious enough to share some honest investing advice with him; unlike his own pyramid scheme sham of a company, my advice was legitimate. Of course, he had nothing to invest with, so I helped him out, the only contingency being that after he made his earnings, which should have been more than enough to pay his debts, he repaid the lenders their initial investment.

As I had anticipated, the street rat was able to make a sizable profit, but instead of paying back those he owed, he took the money given to him and gambled, drank, and partied it away.

Predictable coward that he was, eventually, all he could do was attempt to flee in the end. And so, it came to the day of the harvest." He says, raising a closed fist before my eyes and unfurling his fingers and the rat reappears on his palm, and he closes his fist around it again.

"I can't imagine any creature more befitting to him than this rodent. Whether his greed was justified or not, he never gave anyone else a chance to thrive — it's for the best and for the betterment of my collection. Despite their flaws, I've come to appreciate them all."

My brow quirks, "You've got some pretty weird tastes," I observe.

Aviel merely gives me a half-smile. "Admittedly, my appreciation for them was acquired over time," he replies, his voice coated with an air of mystery. With an almost sadistic glint in his eye, he continues. "I can feel their fear, their desperation. Some cling to the hope of freedom, while others have already given up. I keep them here regardless. Each of them has something to offer me, something of value, and I am not one to let such things go to waste."

"Is that how all their stories go?" I ask.

"They're similar, yes, but of course, there are always outliers." He gives me a pointed look, then tilts his chin up, so I can see a tattoo of the familiar crimson-scaled snake encircling the base of his throat, with her long tail wrapping around his chest. She doesn't move but seems content to rest there.

My eyes widen in recognition. "Lilith," I breathe.

"Not a single one would I ever free, yet in Lilith's case, I'd make an exception. Her only crime was loving a man who despised her and everything she stood for. She alone inspired my sympathy; her total honesty and purity of spirit moved me."

We stay there before the glow of the crackling and hissing fireplace, and I melt into his demonic embrace as he softly recounts the chilling tales about the souls trapped on his skin. It feels strange to seek solace in a demon's arms, and yet Aviel's become my safe space. I find comfort in his embrace.

It seems like the worst thing I can think of is being this taken by a demon until my sister calls my phone well into the night. A menacing figure had appeared outside our apartment, bellowing threats of burning our home and all we held dear to the ground.

Aviel

♥

He is long gone by the time we get there, of course. Leaving a cautionary trail of gasoline as a reminder of his act was a nice touch to the whole thing. The pungent fumes hang thick and low in the air amidst the heavy scents of anxiety and fear, with the tang of adrenaline, and I savor it. But the most intoxicating aroma emanates from Adora, who manages to keep herself contained, but only by all the strength of her will. I close my eyes to better breathe it in.

My fascination with Adora has grown far beyond our casual arrangement, so I need to push things along to take it to the next level. Having Adora for a few hours at a time just isn't enough for me anymore, and there's no way I could ever let on that I'm actually starting to like having her around.

The woman captivates my every thought. I'm awestruck by her beauty, her determination, her kindness. It's a connection past the physical, something deeper and more primal binds us.

Her presence brings a smile to my lips. She challenges me, and moments with her are filled with life and wonder instead of what I realized was stagnation and ennui. Her body is pleasurable beyond my wildest imagination. Add her pure emotions into the mix, and I can easily say she is the best version of them; they entice me blindly, drawing me into her like a moth to a flame.

I find myself wrestling with conflicting desires threatening to savagely tear me apart. Do I crave her safety? Her joy? Her sorrow? Or do I desire her to be ensnared, her essence inextricably tied to me? I'm not sure. I don't care. All I know is that I want her. I *need* her all to myself. And I must do whatever it takes to make her mine.

Alecia is standing on the walkway's pavement just outside their shared apartment. The night sky illuminates her form, her hair pulled back into a sleek ponytail, giving way to a cascade of coils at the bottom, blowing in the wind, her light blue robe billowing around her. Two of Adora's neighbors stand close by, a lanky man and an animated woman, their faces illuminated in an orange glow from the nearby streetlamps. They each wear a look of worry, gathered around Alecia in comfort.

Alecia breaks free from them as we approach, "Adora! Aviel!"

I put on my best look of concern, "We just got word, and came as fast as we were able."

Adora pulls away from me to meet her sister halfway, and the sisters embrace.

"The motherfucker ran off," Alecia mutters, just loud enough for us to hear. Her narrow shoulders sag with exhaustion.

Adora hangs her head in guilt. "I'm so sorry, Alecia. I should have been here." Adora utters. The sisters hug and Alecia shakes her head wearily.

"No, it's all my fault for getting you into this," Alecia says, her voice muffled in Adora's coat.

Their conversation serves as a low-level hum in the background as I inspect the entryway to the apartment—all while never allowing Adora out of my sight.

"Don't say that. It isn't true." Adora scowls, her brow furrowing, "It wasn't your fault that you were sick."

A bitter snort of derision dies in my throat and I almost roll my eyes at the tiresome, never-ending cycle of apologies.

"—We should've just called the damn police!" Adora's next-door neighbor says harshly, the woman looking visibly shaken while the tall, lean male pulls her close to his side.

The collateral damage had been unintentional but necessary; the neighbors would be okay.

Adora and her sister exchange a fleeting glance, uneager to bring attention to their own dealings. Adora shakes her head decisively, her lips pursed with determination. "No." Adora says, her voice firm, "That's not an option right now. Please, don't involve the police just yet."

Alecia concurs with a vehement nod.

"Yeah," Adora's other neighbor, the man, says, shuffling his feet and looking sheepishly up at the sky like he's trying to think of a way not to incriminate himself. "Plus, we just smoked a blunt, so..."

"But what are we gonna do now?"

Adora's brows crease together, and she lets out a deep sigh. She scans our surroundings with an anxious expression before finally meeting my gaze. Her voice is a whisper, as if not wanting to disturb the silence of the night. "Aviel... what should we do?"

I pause for a brief moment and take stock of the situation. Finally, I round on them all, my expression hardening. "Adora, Alecia, you both need to stay with me for a few days," I say sternly, "Noone would dare threaten you in my home. I'll have my assistant send over a couple of security people. They'll keep things in order, and, if he comes back again, we'll have to take matters into our own hands. They will be able to handle this without police interference and keep it completely confidential."

Like a challenge, I look each one of them in the eye: Alecia; Adora's neighbors; Adora herself and receive no objections in return. After a short while, they all nod at me, accepting my decision—as if they had any other option.

Adora's face melts into a look of sweet relief. Her eyes meet mine and without a word, she reaches out to me. I step forward and wrap my arms around her frame as she tightly clutches onto me like a lifeline, head resting on my chest in relief and trust unknowingly placed within me. The warmth of her body radiates into me, and I'm filled with a pure sensation, something I've never felt before and can't even begin to explain. But even that elation pales in comparison to the feeling of having Adora. For a moment, all that exists is her.

I take a deep breath and inhale the sweet aroma of Adora's hair, and in my embrace, I feel her start to relax - ever so slightly. Alecia takes an uncertain step towards us, but it is only then that I pull away from Adora, as if waking up.

"Thank you," Alecia whispers, and if I were the least bit human then perhaps I would feel a sliver of guilt.

But I'm only happy that my plan is working, and I hadn't even needed to do much. While Adora and Alecia are away, the neighbors will be vigilant of any suspicious activity around the apartments, my security will keep watch from outside—not that they need to—and the sisters will come with me. All I want is Adora, but Alecia is a small price to pay for that.

I stand before the pair of neighbors now, and a grimace spreads across my features as I say, "Unfortunate that we meet properly under such circumstances." It's an understatement. I'm burning with the desire to grab Adora, force her into my car, and drive away, only decorum demands that I remain.

"Yeah," The bespectacled one named Tayo steps forward to shake my hand, his glasses like two narrow windows into his soul. "We'll have to introduce ourselves properly after this is all over."

The woman, Helen, follows suit. "It's nice to..." Suddenly she cuts herself off mid-sentence and stares at me with glassy, reddened eyes a while longer, seeming to sense something she can't quite express, and if she has some privileged glimpse of my true nature then it doesn't matter. She is silent for a few moments before finally saying, "God, I shouldn't of smoked up tonight," she shakes her head before she gives me an appreciative smile: "Thanks for taking care of our girls, Aviel."

"It's what anyone in my position would do," I reply smoothly, with a dip of my head. But that's not true; I wanted Adora from the moment I saw her and this was the only for me to have her.

I call ahead to have my assistant, Jerry, prepare the guest room for Alecia, and Adora doesn't protest to joining me in my chambers. This is checkmate I suppose, and my sweet Adora is none the wiser.

The sun filters through my bedroom windows, casting a golden hue as I watch Jones lead Alecia away to escort her to a doctor's appointment. I let Adora stew in my study, job hunting on her laptop for an opportunity to land her feet. I can almost taste a bitterness on my tongue as I contemplate the necessity of crushing her fragile little dreams once again.

Such a persistent woman.

I can't deny the temptation of playing the part of her valiant knight and saving her from her pain.

I fight back the urge to go and watch her while she works; I know my fixation on her is worsening. It doesn't help that I can sense her anxiety filling the entire house like a fog, it's suffocating, and it makes me want to strip her naked and delve deep within her.

The raging temptation finally overpowering me, I go to the study where she is typing away, and when she looks up as I enter and her lips tug up into a subtle smile, I know I'm going to have her and bury myself so far inside of her that she won't ever be able to get rid of me.

"Hey," Adora says softly as I settle close behind her.

"Are you almost done?" I reply with an arched brow, all the while wondering why, for some inexplicable reason, I am matching the hushed intonation of her voice.

She twists around in her seat, our eyes connecting like magnets, "Do you know any demons who can pull a few strings to land me a job?" She chuckles at her own joke, her laughter is like a spell and I find myself transfixed by her soft lips.

Managing to drag my gaze away, I reply, "Be careful or you may come to rely on me for all your needs."

Her smile only grows wider, and she rises up from her seat to loop her arms around my neck. "Would that be such a bad thing?" She whispers sweetly, her breath hot on my skin.

I back away to trace my finger along the soft outline of her face and feel the shiver race through her body. "Naughty human," I sneer, bringing my face close to hers until our noses almost touch. I can feel the electricity coursing between us, and I bite back a smile. "You must be hungry, let's go somewhere for dinner before you conjure up more trouble."

Her eyes light up with anticipation, her enthusiasm sending an unexpected spark through me, "Is this a date?" she breathes.

I roll my eyes. "No. Just food. And if you're good," I purr, "Maybe I'll finally give you what you've been craving for so long."

Her mouth snaps shut. Now that I have her attention, she won't dare bring up this date nonsense again.

Aviel is a paradox of romance and enigma that I still can't quite decipher; he hadn't said a word, but he had prepared for me several outfit choices and dainty VVS diamond drop earrings to finish the ensemble for our non-date, 'Just Food' outing. All of them perfectly fit and suited to my tastes.

I glide towards Aviel's bedroom door in a fitted velvet midi dress of a deep burgundy hue, my matching suede block heels clicking as I make my way out. As I cross the threshold, I hear Alecia's voice in the hall.

“Okay! Look at you, miss thing!” I give a little twirl in my new clothes and shoes, feeling sexy and confident, appreciative of her gassing me up. Alecia quirks her lips in amusement, and we embrace.

"Thanks, but I don't know what to say," I said, gesturing to my attire. "How on earth could he have known?"

"Well...Aviel did come to me this morning and asked what I thought you'd like," she reveals.

Startled, I blink, "Really?" The sweet gesture catches me off guard, "Boujie and just a little thotty, it’s perfect— I should've known."

"You know I got you." Alecia says with a wink, "He won’t be able to take his eyes off of you tonight."

A sliver of doubt comes into my mind, “He said it’s not a date, just food.”

“Please,” Alecia says, “We all know that men don't do romantic dinner outings with women that they aren't attracted to and want to impress, don't play. Oh!— And he even got something for your girl," she then turns her head, and her earrings swing gracefully, their movements almost like a dance.

I pull one of the slender wires, and the teardrop jewels catch the light. "From Aviel?" I breathe.

“Our friend's got game,” she grins.

"Speaking of..." I bit my lip and blurt out, "Do you think I'm being played?" I don't know why I ask; there's something in me that needs to verbalize a nagging doubt that I can't seem to shake.

Alecia sighs, "Listen, Adora, that's always a possibility in any relationship, right? But you can't let fear hold you back from taking a chance. Enjoy yourself in the moment for what it is. It might not last forever, but if you don't give it a chance, you'll never know what could have been." she smiles at me warmly, "I'm glad he's taking you out tonight; you've been on an emotional rollercoaster for a minute. You deserve it."

I breathe a little easier, knowing that I can always trust Alecia to be real with me.

"Thanks," I say, hugging her appreciatively,

She tightens the embrace and whispers, "Thank Aviel, not me." I glance up and can't help but smile as I raise my chin and take in the sight of him, finding him leaning against the wall further down the hall, admiring me in my new dress. Alecia turns with me.

Aviel looks stunning in a sophisticated dark Armani tuxedo, a clean-cut burgundy dress shirt, and a burgundy pocket square; his hair combed back in a dignified sweep. His appearance exudes an overwhelming amount of magnetism, drawing me in yet freezing me on spot.

Alecia leans in and murmurs, "You legit need to snag him, so go get him..." Before I can even respond, she nudges me forward in Aviel's direction.

He levels a gaze at me that sends electricity through my veins.

Taking a deep breath, I walk up to him and murmur, “Hey you,” I gaze up at him, "Am I up to code?"

He takes a step forward and rests his hand on the small of my back. My body shivers at his closeness, wetness inflaming my core.

His eyes take me in from head to toe as he reaches out and takes my hand in his. His lips part and a breath-taking smirk edges into his features, "I'd like a little more access," He leans forward and rumbles into my ear. "But in this dress... leave it to you to impress without trying." he breathed out in an almost reverent way.

Alecia appears beside us both, "Have her back home by twelve." She points a stern finger, but the cheeky grin gives her away.

"What, you mean *my* home?" he says without missing a beat, quirking an eyebrow. "We'll be back before you know it. For now, you just order whatever you like."

"Y'all have a good time." She says without another moment's delay before retreating to the guest room.

Once she departs, Aviel pauses, his smile going a little crooked. He seizes me and shocks me yet again, capturing my lips with a force and conviction that leaves me breathless. I melt into his embrace, and the world around us falls away. His lips leave a trail of fire as they traverse my neck, sending waves of pleasure through my body. He kisses me to the depths of my soul without any sign of relenting, his fervor only growing as he claims me in a passionate display of dominance. When he finally pulls back from our kiss, I feel exhausted by the power of it.

For a while, he studies me intently, and I'm lost in the fathomless depths of his eyes. His hold tightens around my waist, and his eyes darken as though warning that there's much more of this to come. A moment later, the spell is broken with a gentle smile from him. "Shall we?"

"We shall," I say, my legs still wobbly from our ferocious embrace. Aviel snakes an arm around my waist and steers me out of the house towards his sleek Sedan.

We draw stares from the onlookers as we walk into a charming little Italian spot nestled in the heart of the city, arm-in-arm. The atmosphere is awash with a warm candlelit ambiance, and warm yellow lights cast a sparkly glow onto the walls of white stucco and exposed brick rough-hewn stone, with centuries-old brickwork adding character and charm.

Aviel is the perfect gentleman throughout our non-date, and over a plate of succulent shrimp scampi and glasses of white wine, he probes further into me. At some point, with my lips lubricated with liquor, I eventually tell him about Alecia raising me after our parents passed in a car accident. She had to leave school and find cheap housing for us, working two jobs to support us. The housing development project I had been working on was so important to me because it would help vulnerable families just like ours.

"To make lives easier." I say, tracing the rim of my glass with a finger, "It was kind of my way of paying it forward, I guess."

Aviel watches me with a certain look in his eyes. His gaze is almost too intense for the moment, and I feel myself warm up under its scrutiny. "You have a beautiful heart, Adora." He says softly.

I exhale a breath at his gracious compliment, completely taken aback. His words gently warm my heart, and I feel something else stir inside me besides attraction, admiration, or respect – it's an emotion deeper than all of those combined.

"So, do you have a past?" I ask him. "Beyond..." I gesture to his tattooed hands.

I find out that though he and his father had a falling out, he wished him no ill will. He never knew his mother — a fact that seemed to haunt him more than he would ever admit.

He reveals to me, for the first time, bits and pieces of his own past. He changed his appearance and relocated every thirty years because there was a time when hostile humans had tried to hunt him down after noticing that he didn't age. It was a long time ago, but he hadn't forgotten it.

It's the most he had ever told me about his own past, and I begin to understand more of why he is the way he is.

"So, you've never been in love?" Is my final question.

"I have no heart, which makes you humans capable of what you call love," he replies stoically, regarding me with hooded eyes from across the table.

"You really believe that?" I press on.

He nods, and I feel sad for him. I come to realize why love is just as foreign to him as it is for me to comprehend the sinister aspects of his world. How can anyone live for so long and never experience love? Sure, love can bring heartbreak and suffering, but it makes life worth living. I can't imagine not caring for my sister or even not caring for Aviel. And though I admire his tenacious autonomy being so isolated from the world of emotions, his words also make me acutely aware of my own feelings—how could I have been so foolish that I let myself fall into the abyss with this man? By grasping him more clearly, I'm starting to recognize my own error too late.

I have feelings for Aviel; against all odds, this demon has made me fall for him. And I feel a sting in my chest as I come to acknowledge that he would never feel the same way.

In my trance-like state, it only hits me that I left my purse back at the restaurant once we're in the car and about to leave.

"It's fine, just wait here; I'll get it for you," Aviel says, ever the savior, leaving me in the still-running car.

While Aviel heads back to get it, I wait, surrounded by the idling engine's low purr, watching his silhouette as it diminishes beyond the pale white glow of the headlights.

A heavy fog had descended, the near-empty parking lot eerily still and silent.

Perhaps it's just being in an unfamiliar place; today is only my second time in Aviel's own car, which he admitted to never driving much, its leather seats and satin interiors near pristine. I'm more used to John's non-descript vehicle—heck, strange as it is; for a while, I was used to being blindfolded when heading to Aviel's.

I allow my mind to wander freely and give myself the rare luxury of indulging in the day's events, but I can't help an odd feeling that I can't quite place sitting on my shoulders like a weight.

That's when I hear it; a faint vibration - coming from his glove compartment, completely interrupting my train of thought. Curious, I pull on the latch so it falls open; inside, a lone cell phone glows at me from its pocket of darkness. I could have sworn that Aviel had his phone on him. So what can this be?

Picking it up, I rotate it in my hands to peer at the screen, and for a moment, nothing happens. No notifications, messages, or anything at all save for a weather forecast news app, and all seems quiet until a new text notification pops up:

'It was a pleasure, boss, hope the gal is worth every penny.'

My mind blanks for a moment as the text stares back at me, and I'm too stunned to even move.

The hair on my arms rises like all my senses are suddenly alert and tuned into danger. Everything around me seems sharper and more defined, like I'm waking up from a deep sleep.

I have a bad feeling about this, and I know Aviel will be back any minute.

I snatch up my phone from my lap with nervous haste, feeling the heat and weight of it in my hand as I dial his number. I hold the phone to my ear, listening intently—half wondering if this strange new device I've just found will ring.

It doesn't. But Aviel picks up after just a few rings, and my gut tightens. I nearly stammer as I try to speak, "Aviel, where are you?"

"Just about to leave; why?" His reply comes back crisply.

"Wait—" I hesitate, biting my lip, "While you're in there, can you grab me another slice of that tiramisu? I liked it; I want Alecia to try it too." A beat passes as I hold my breath waiting for his response, hoping he will acquiesce.

Finally, Aviel utters a defeated sigh, "Cake for Alecia. Anything else?"

"No, that's it." My breath is a ghostly whisper in the silence. "Thanks."

"I'll be back soon," he replies.

"See you then," I whisper—yanking the phone away from my ear in one swift motion, ending the call, and setting it down again.

My hand trembles as I retrieve the new device and open the message thread, a million questions running through my head that demand answers. But I can't help dreading what will be revealed there.

"The gal"? What else is Aviel involved in?

And as I read the messages, I feel nausea rise from the pit of my stomach. I find another string of exchanges between Aviel and one D. McCloud, and further back are messages from another contact, Nancy. My heart skips a beat as I start to fit the pieces of the puzzle together.

It's beyond too late when my mind finally registers the crunch of gravel beneath slow footfalls just outside, shattering the stillness. The driver-side door yanks open, and I jerk my head up with a startled gasp to meet Aviel's darkening eyes before his gaze shifts to what is in my hands.

A muscle in his jaw clenches, and for a few seconds, there is only silence.

"Adora," he says at last, his voice nearly a whisper. "What are you doing?"

I meet his abyssal gaze with a fiery glare before dropping my gaze to the strange phone in my grasp. Clutching the wretched thing that links me to all of this, I retort with indignation, "Me? Why don't you explain why your people are updating you on hacking my financial data or sniping my investors? Visiting my office?... Threatening my sister?" My voice catches on the last words.

Aviel is silent for a moment, his features softening ever so slightly, "Adora..."

"My sister was terrified for her life, Aviel! I lost my fucking job, my dream project's been thrown away—" I'm trembling hard, and I struggle to even get the words out around the lump in my throat. "And all this time, you were just playing in my face, while this was all your doing? Your fault?! Why! I trusted you!"

I see his eyes close briefly, and his lips press together before he answers, "That was your choice, Adora. You can't be so naive to think that I am some heroic knight."

I glare at him, my throat burning with barely-contained rage, and tears fill my eyes. I want to scream at him and call him a manipulative liar, but all that comes out is a raspy whisper, "No, not a knight..." I agree with a shake of my head and almost chuckle. "You'd have to be human to be that."

Disgusted, I throw the phone on the driver's seat and avert my gaze away from him to stare out the window through bleary eyes, unable to even stomach looking at his face at this point. "Drive me back. We're more than done here."

After several failed attempts to engage me, Aviel sits back in his seat, and we drive back in deathly silence. There's no point in talking anyway. What more is there to say? The distant sounds of traffic provide the only ambiance to the heavy atmosphere in the car, and once we arrive, I scoop up my purse and leave the cake behind. It only takes me fifteen minutes to pack my stuff and leave with my sister without so much as a goodbye. Since we aren't in any danger, there's no reason for us not to return home.

Aviel was right, he was what he was, nothing more than a monster in human skin, and I had been stupid to trust him despite him being every red flag on the damn map.

I can say, at least one good thing has come out of it all, my sister is alive and well. I'd consider my broken heart a fair payment.

Aviel

I clench my teeth and glare at my assistant, seething with anger.

"There isn't much I can do; I've tried calling her fifty-five times, sir," he says.

"Then call her fifty-six times!" I hiss, my voice dripping with venom as I stare daggers at him.

"You have to face it. She doesn't want to talk. She's blocked your number," he adds in a mutter, "...and mine."

Patience evaporating, I clench my jaw and glare at him, wondering if it's too early to give Lilith a snack after her last meal. What good is an assistant if he can't even assist? I've never felt so frustrated in my life, and Adora is doing a damn good job of testing my patience and pushing me to the brink of insanity.

Jep clears his throat, and I want to reach out and wring his neck for even suggesting what he was about to say, "Perhaps you should think about going there to apologize; tell her how you feel." he suggests cautiously.

I scoff incredulously. Apologize? I've never apologized a day in my life, and what is he going on about *feelings*? I'm incapable of such human trivialities. Those are things that I have no use for whatsoever.

"I'll arrange for some flowers to be sent to her house ahead of your arrival." Jake offers stiffly, crossing to the other side of the meeting room.

"I am not—" I snarl in defiance, but Jethro abruptly shuts me down with cold, unmistakable finality.

"*You are welcome, sir.*" he firmly closes the door behind him before I can retaliate, and I can't help but marvel at his audacity.

That presumptuous, smug bastard.

"Fancy a meal, Lilith?" I inquire as she gracefully scales my body and coils herself around my lap. I run the back of my hand along her back.

Lilith raises her head, and with blinding speed, she lunges forward and clamps into the flesh of my shoulder, narrowly missing my throat, her fangs sinking in deep. The pain is wicked, and cursing, I pry her away. No sooner had I wrenched her off than she is back again, lacerating my hand this time, leaving two deep bloody gashes.

I glared into her eyes, two smoldering pits of unfettered wrath, and I can't help but gasp in disbelief, "You too? After all this time...you are complicit in this betrayal?" Fury boils in my veins, and she hisses her defiance in response, clearly pleased with her own treachery.

"I will *not* lower myself to the level of a human!" I sneer.

Lilith rises up before me and locks her eyes with mine, her gaze intense and unyielding, her burning eyes searching deep into mine. She isn't going to let me off the hook until I face this truth head-on—I've allowed myself to fall for a human, one who makes me smile and, dare I say it, fulfills me, who touches something within me that had long been dormant.

I crave Adora—and not because of what I can get from her—but because of what she does to me. No one has ever made me feel such affection and fear all at once.

I long for her, and I want her to stay with me more than anything else. I lust for her emotions just as I am in awe of them. Never in my long existence have I been so tormented by a human, I want her so ferociously that it terrifies me. Whatever it is humans feel for one another, I've somehow found myself on that level.

A sinister whisper resonates in the back of my mind, urging me to trap Adora in an eternal prison, taking what is rightfully mine. But I scorn the thought. I'd been determined to play a dangerous game on my terms, and yet, here I am, defeated. She's gone, leaving only regret, a heavy burden I bear as I ponder the lesson I've learned too late.

My throat tightens, constricting my airways as Lilith leaves me. I'm not sure what I am to do with this new revelation. Fear and desperation swell within me. I'm a demon, a creature of the abyss, and not a man. Adora emanates a heavenly luminosity while I am draped in inky night, but for a moment, we were intertwined, our differences mysteriously forgotten.

But I don't know how to get to that place with her again; I have no clue what to do to win a woman's heart. I try to think of what they do during that absurd love holiday of theirs, but nothing seems even remotely suitable for this situation. There is only one thing I can do, and that is to give her my truth.

My hand darts towards the only shirt I can find, and I hastily thrust it over myself, despite the fact that my wounded body leaks deep crimson through the fabric. I depart, ready to bring my precious, silly human back home to where she truly belongs — in my arms.

I rap my knuckles against Adora's apartment door and wait with bated breath for someone to answer, only to deflate when Alecia appears, her eyes bearing the weight of a thousand daggers.

She looks me up and down, then in a venomous flash, slams the door in my face.

I stand motionless and let out a deep sigh before I knock again. This time more urgently.

The door opens a crack this time, "May I help your trifling ass?" Alecia snarls coldly, not bothering to mask the scorn radiating beneath.

I take a calming breath and explain the reason for my unannounced arrival. "Is Adora home?" I ask, and I hate how I can't help the anticipation in my tone.

She folds her arms over her chest and sneers contemptuously, "She doesn't want to see you." She shoves the door with all her might—which really isn't much, but I bat it open again, the force of it reverberating throughout the room, echoing her disdain.

I take a deep breath and square my shoulders, "Look, if she doesn't want to see me, then she can tell me that herself." I say firmly, my determination steeled by a burning in my chest.

The response comes flatly and instantly, "I don't want to see you."

I look up from Alecia's face to find Adora, her eyes piercing me with righteous fury, sharp and icy. Each word slams into me like a punch to the gut.

"There you have it, bye. Have the day you deserve—oh, and I'm keeping the earrings." Alecia reaches for the door handle for the last time to shut it in my face, and beyond her, I see Adora begin to turn away, sending a bone-deep hurt resonating through my soul.

I have to see her, to talk to her—even a moment would make all the difference. Adrenaline flows through me, urging me forward on my quest to see her. I thrust my foot into the door frame, halting its closure, and force my way in, ignoring Alecia's startled protests and grumbled curses in my wake.

The atmosphere shifts upon my entry; the air between us pregnant with mounting tension.

Adora whirls around to face me, "What the hell do you think you're doing?" she ices me through narrowed eyes.

But beyond the scent of her anger, there is an abyss of pain radiating with hurt so thick it nearly chokes me. She looks a shadow of herself, as if all life had been stolen from her—have I done this to her? Was the last time I saw her really just a few short days ago? It seems as if a lifetime has passed since the night she left. I stand rooted to the spot, and for a moment of weakness, I wonder if there is anything left to be salvaged between us.

"I..." My words trail off into silence.

She's right. What the hell am I doing?

Alecia steps out from behind me, her hands firmly planted on her hips. She throws a dagger-like glance at me before turning back to her sister.

"You need me to call the police?" she asks Adora, and I almost scoff out loud. As if human police officers have any chance against a demon bursting with raw power.

"What a bad idea," I say before I can stop myself, my voice carrying a little louder than I had intended.

Alecia ices me again. "Come again?"

"No, I got this," Adora replies calmly, her voice betraying a deep resolve. "I'll handle him. Alone."

Alecia hesitates for a moment, before finally relenting to Adora's demand. "I'll be in the next room if he needs a reminder where the door is," she says to Adora, finally turning away and heading towards her room, but not before throwing one final, menacing look at me. It would have been lethal if I weren't immortal.

The door slams shut, cutting off the sound of her departing steps, and my eyes are drawn to the large bouquet of red roses lying atop the coffee table. A part of me wonders why they are still in their plastic jacket—and then something in me leaps with hope. Before I can fully process this, Adora's gaze follows mine, her muddled emotions flitting across her features like a storm.

"Your assistant brought them over..." She whispers, "I forgive him." Then her eyes lock onto mine, and I feel my soul bared before her as she adds with icy disdain, "Not you."

With a sigh, I begin, "Adora...."

Her response is scathing. "What?" she snaps. "What can you possibly say now?"

I reply evenly, "If you would just let me speak—"

"Haven't you said enough already? You were right; I was stupid to trust you. I'll hold that L. I shouldn't have expected anything more from you; it's in your nature. Now, why don't you just go."

The sheer pain and anger emanating from her fill the room, and I realize I am witnessing the full torrent of emotion that she has kept in check for far too long. For a while, I'm rendered speechless. Despite everything, she's still the most breathtaking woman I've ever seen.

She gives me a dismissing once over before declaring, "You fucked up, and you look fucking horrible, by the way."

"It's been a rough couple of days," I confess without anger or defense. I'm willing to take anything she throws at me as long as we can get somewhere. Maybe then, hopefully, she can see that and understand my reasons.

My eyes remain fixed on her. "Just five minutes, Adora, and then I'll leave," I say firmly, "I promise."

"You have two," she crosses her arms tightly across her chest. "Start talking."

My head is pounding. I have mere moments to explain. I begin cautiously, "I only did what I did to keep you—"

"You could have had me without the mind games," Adora interjects, chopping my sentence off at the head. "Nice try, though."

I shake my head, desperately trying to make her grasp my point. "No, you don't understand. I don't think the way you do—"

"More like you don't think at all," she sneers back.

"You can't keep cutting me off when I only have two minutes," I grit out between clenched teeth, and the vein on my neck pulses in my ineffectual attempt to force my composure back into place.

She retaliates just as fiercely, "And you can't do what you did to me and expect me to be okay with it!"

I give in, "Fine, you're right."

She stares at me, her anger radiating off her body. "Exactly." she says, "So now, you've got thirty seconds."

"Thirty sec-?!" My mind races with panic and rage as I count down her ultimatum in my head.

"Twenty-nine!"

I curse myself for allowing my temper to get the better of me as I start from the beginning, choosing my words more carefully this time. "Please, just...hear me out."

She stands there in silent expectation, waiting for an explanation that can undo everything that has been done—an unattainable feat.

I gather my bearings, prepared to bargain, "I wired all the money back—"

"It's not about the money!" She shouts, and her rage shocks through my body like ten thousand volts.

My stomach drops as she storms away from me and towards the kitchen. I follow her through the doorway and watch her pour herself a glass of water which she doesn't drink.

My words seem inadequate, and I'm so painfully aware of the growing distance between us. I have to do something. "The truth is I'm horrible at this."

She only continues to stare into the water.

Desperate, I continue, my voice strained and hoarse, "I hate that I've ruined everything we could have had beyond repair and that I've hurt you and your sister in the process..."

"And took my livelihood," she mutters, but still doesn't look up at me.

“And that.”

“Ruined years of work creating a shell company just to compete with me. Who fucking does that?”

"I know, I did all of that." Lost, I pause to pull in a breath, "And I don't know what I can say to make this all better—"

"How about 'I'm sorry!'"

"Fine, I'm sorry!" I slam my fist on the counter in frustration but go quiet as soon as the sound ripples through the air. "I'm sorry," I repeat, softer this time, finally breaking the silence we fall into with a deep sigh.

I rake a hand through my hair, struggling to meet her gaze. "I should have been the one to send those roses," I admit eventually, my shoulders sagging in defeat.

"Yeah, John shouldn't have had to apologize on your behalf."

My brows furrow in confusion as I try to recall the face to match the name. "Who's John?"

"Your assistant." She supplies dryly with the most condescending tone she can muster.

"Hm," I say with a click of my tongue, "I always thought his name was Joel..."

The corner of her mouth curls up slightly as I let out a soft chuckle. I exhale deeply, searching for the courage to keep going.

"So, I don't know my assistant's name. I don't know how to ap ologize...or how to feel and express emotions like you do." My chest constricts, and my mouth turns arid as I listen to myself speak. The words escape me. "What I did know is that I needed you—even if I didn't deserve you—and I did whatever I could to keep you because I wanted you to need me too."

Adora regards me coolly. "You fucked up bad, Aviel," she says, her voice hard, "You tried to manipulate me into being with you. You lied to me."

A palpable tension thickens between us as if her words were a volley of arrows that have lodged themselves directly through my being.

I nod, my throat tight. "I know," I say. "I didn't want to lose you. And before you say I could have just asked, I don't know how to do that either. I don't know how to be anything else other than what I am." I ache as I speak, dreading the response to follow, yet needing to hear it.

"What you are," she enunciates slowly and deliberately, "Not who you are." She let's out a heavy sigh and continues, "I know *what* you are, Aviel, and in some ways, I don't expect you to be any different. But you can still be a demon who apologizes, a demon who asks, and a demon who feels."

I feel unfounded hope flare within me, almost paralyzing me with its intensity. "That doesn't make sense, but let's go with it." I encourage her.

She laughs and placed a hand over her heart. "The heart doesn't feel, Aviel. My sister has a different heart now, and she's exactly the same. Maybe a human's and demon's soul have their own manner of being too. I only expect you to be the best authentic version of yourself."

"Even if that version feels fear?" I murmur, my gaze slipping from hers.

"I thought you said—"

My gaze snaps back to hers, "I know what I said, but a part of me was —is— afraid to lose you, which is why I devised to keep you. A part of me dreaded that I'll never get to see you, or touch you, or hear your voice again. That's why I'm here. And another part of me is afraid that I will change into something I can't recognize, which is why I can't be any different."

Like a soft breeze, she approaches me and hugged me tightly, filling my being with a warmth different from my own. Maybe different isn't so bad after all, I think to myself as I learn to embrace it.

"I forgive you..." Adora says softly, "But I don't know if I want you back."

The words make me stiffen in her hold, but her arms wrap around me tighter, and I'm frozen in her warmth, my mind struggling to understand what she's saying.

Eventually, she pulls away and stares me down for what feels like forever before saying anything. "You need to understand, I'm not going to be with someone who tries to manipulate me." she says, her voice stern and her eyes solemn.

"You have all the right in the world to reject me," I mutter in return with a bitter scoff, "considering what I've done."

"So, is that it?" She interrogates frostily.

As I am about to give a cursory reply, it slowly dawns on me that Adora is giving me one last opportunity to keep her, to choose to have her of her own volition instead of entrapping her—an offer tinged with danger and inconvenience that goes completely against my better judgement—but the only way I could have her.

And in so few words, she's telling me that if I don't do anything, I'm already giving her reason to reject me. I want to fight against my nature for her.

A newfound courage surges through my veins, "No," I declare. "That isn't it."

I lower myself to one knee, then the other, under the burden of my own guilt, and my overwhelming want for her. Releasing my pride, I embrace her possessively by the waist, burying my face in her warmth, feeling her shudder with emotion against me before I raise my eyes to lock with her own.

I firmly state one more thing."I need you back, Adora. You're the most beautiful, incredible, resillient woman I've ever met. I need you to give me a chance to prove myself to you—I'll do whatever it takes. I'll make sure you won't regret it."

"And you'll do anything?" Adora says. "Even if I expect you to give me cuddles whenever I want them, or to text me three times a day, go on a legitimate date once a week, minimum?"

I respond without hesitation, my throat tight with a sincere intensity. "Did I not make myself clear? Anything." I reply, my voice raw and void of all pretense. "I won't lie and say it will be easy, but I'm willing to do whatever it takes."

When she sees I am steadfast in my resolve, a radiant smile stretches across her lips. "Okay then, it's a deal." Adora says finally; she tugs her phone out of her pocket, levels the camera, and snaps a photo of me before I can react.

I groan warily. "What are you scheming now?" I grumble, rising to my feet.

"Documenting this moment," Adora grins mischievously. "John wanted a photo of when you groveled on your knees."

"Fucking John." I roll my eyes, "If you send that to him, I'll be forced to kill him." I say, but I can't help but feel a sense of affection for her. She has a way of making even the most humiliating moments feel not so bad. "I suppose I'll need to thank him, and apologize to your sister."

"Sounds like a fun apology tour." Adora giggles, pressing her forehead against my chest. I take a deep breath and hold her close, realizing that despite how irritating this situation is to me—-the power of Adora's warmth still manages to make me smile.

"I won't disappoint you, Adora." I tell her softly, "I promise."

"I love you too," she whispers into my chest.

"I never said—"

Adora turns her face up to look at me. She placed her finger on my lips to hush me up. "Shh, let's just go with it."

I smile and hugged her back before kissing the top of her head. Love is an understatement to what I feel for her but who was I to argue with the creatures who had invented it.

"My silly human," I murmur.

I sit hunkered down in the home office, my fingers flying over the keyboard as I hurry to confirm that the last of the materials for Redevelopment Solutions' housing development project are sourced and green. It is coming along nicely, and I find I have a lot more say over its progress than I initially ever did, so much so that I never did end up accepting my job back from Lewis & Co., who Aviel made sure couldn't crucify Keystone, nor Redevelopment Solutions for any claims of greenwashing after they went public about the old CEO's poor business practices, and our commitment to change things going forward. There would be quite a bit of renovating to be done.

It was a part of Aviel's reconciliation with me, and he was true to his word, leaving me in charge of the development project of my dreams that I can have my say over.

I glance up as the study doors creak open, revealing a grimacing Aviel laden with bouquets of flowers, two gift bags, and an enormous stuffed pink bear draped over his shoulder. It seems John has the day off; otherwise, he'd probably be relegated to the task. The man deserved the vacation.

"Happy Valentine's Day," Aviel grumbles.

I can't hold back my grin, "You look so convincing." I say, rising from my seat and circling around the desk to greet him.

He grunts, inching closer with gritted teeth, "Take them before I change my mind," he replies, pushing the bags into my hands; before I can respond, he proceeds to set the bear on one of the armchairs. "The other is for Alecia. Just check the tags there."

I glance up at him, peering past his grim exterior to see his true self; a man who had cared enough to remember my sister, and it makes me feel all marshmallowy inside. I stand on my toes and give him a kiss on the cheek before setting the bags on the desk.

I open mine and gasp when I see what was in it; the perfect gift. "Aviel, I love it!" I turn and hug him before he can protest, then cradle the velvet box with a pink diamond heart necklace to my chest. For someone with no heart at all, he sure knows the way to mine.

I catch him gazing at me, his eyes soft now, and the crease lines between his brows from a few moments earlier become faint. Something about that look in his eyes makes my heart flutter like a butterfly's wings.

"Love suits you," I whisper, leaning into him.

"I know you like your Valentine's Day," he says, grabbing my hand and kissing the back of it.

I put my gift bag down to peek at Alecia's present. "So, what's this?"

Inside is a small wrapped box and a red envelope on top, so I have no idea what it is.

"It's that perfume that she likes and two tickets to go and watch a basketball game. A friend of a friend asked if you had a sister. He'd like to take her on a date."

"They're...human, right?" I ask tentatively.

Aviel's eyes become impossibly darker, and now it's his turn to grin. "Not in the least." He whispers, his voice low and sultry, sending a shiver through me.

I raise my eyebrow at that, and he closes the space between us to lock his arms around me possessively, pressing his hard body against mine. His lips, soft as satin, skim along my jaw and down the side of my neck, making my body tingle with anticipation.

His hands drift slowly down my waist to the curve of my hips. "We have a few more hours before we have to meet your insufferable friends..." His lips move against my skin as he speaks, and I have to force myself to concentrate on his words instead of giving into my desire to be consumed by the sensation. "But before that, I want to hear you scream my name," he growls in my ear, sending another wave of heat coursing through me.

My pulse quickens and I cling to him for support as my breath hitches with anticipation. One more kiss on my neck, and I'm gone—lost in his encompassing embrace, lost in the moment, lost in him. I gasp in blissful delight as he sweeps me into his chamber.

There, his hands take possession of me, skimming the fabric of my clothing and tugging until it drops away, revealing my bare skin to him. I quiver with anticipation as his fingertips trace an intimate path on my skin. Our eyes lock, and the energy between us is palpable.

I slowly peel his shirt away, watching as each sinew on his body is illuminated in the dusky light, revealing the bold artwork adorning his toned body. I never get tired of looking at him, the designs that move across his skin still entrance me, and my fingertips ache to trace the shapes and hues, to feel the art that dances on his skin.

If someone had told me a year ago that I would be making love to a demon on Valentine's Day, I would have called them insane. Now, I can't fathom my life without this captivating man. His touch sends electric intensity rushing through my body, leaving me wanting more. Do I love him in spite of his infernal nature or because of it? All I know is that I love him immeasurably; nothing could ever change that now.

My eyes wander the detailed designs on his skin until they come to rest on one that causes a flutter in my chest. Etched in black and grey, curling cursive letters spelled one word – my name – and as I reach out to touch it, the movement of all the others cease.

"It means I'm yours?" I whisper.

"And," He says, cupping a hand around the nape of my neck and pulling me to him. "It also means I'm yours."

My body trembles with emotion, and before I know it, tears are welling up in my eyes, then streaming down my face. Aviel brushes them away with a tenderness that surprises me.

"Silly human, don't cry..." he murmurs, an alluring smirk on his lips, and hypnotic gaze drawing me helplessly into him. "Not until I'm inside of you."

He claims me with a passionate kiss, replacing the shock of tearful joy with pleasure as his lips meet mine. I kiss him back with fervor, the salty taste of my tears mixing in with the sweet flavor of his lips. His most authentic self, and it's all for me.

His grip digs into me with new intensity, and I draw in a sharp breath as he hoists me off my feet, my legs instinctively wrapping around him. Aviel lays me onto the expanse of red and black sheets of the large four-poster bed, never breaking our kiss nor relinquishing his hold on my body.

Now his kiss is demanding, full of passion and desire that we both feel acutely; two halves of one whole coming together to form something entirely new, something entirely its own.

Aviel's expert hands explore my body with a knowledge that surpasses my own, slowly making their way down the flat plane of my stomach, to my thighs, to where I'm already damp and pining for more. His finger enters me at the same time his tongue dances into my mouth, tangling with mine, and I welcome him, tiny whimpers escaping my lips around our kiss.

Bringing his thumb up to circle my clit, he elicits shudders from my body, drawing out pleasure like he has an eternity. The slow, torturous circles make me cling to him desperately, eager for everything he can give, and as a raspy moan escapes me, his teeth sink into the fullness of my lower lip, almost breaking the skin and tugs, coaxing an involuntary arch of my back in a silent plea for more.

My passion only inflames his own, and he responds with one more teasing stroke of my clit before dragging himself away from my lips to the crook of my neck, over my breasts, and finally, Aviel slides down my body, luxurious and slow, against my aching flesh.

Taking in the scent of my arousal, his eyes darken with desire, and his hungry moan reverberates deep within me as he buries himself between my thighs. Prying my thighs wide for him, he hovers over me; his hot breath whispers against my sex, and I strain against the sheets, desperate for his touch, pleading silently for him to take me.

My senses ignite as his tongue plunges between my slick lips, teasing and tasting me in time with a new rhythm of his fingers that tease at my clit and send shocks of unbridled pleasure rushing through me. He devours me, exploring my heated depths, absorbing every sound and shudder made in response. His tongue and fingers send me spiraling to new heights, and I close my eyes and surrender to the sensations, only to hear a loud hiss. When I open them again, it's to see Lilith is halfway off Aviel's skin, perched on his shoulder and looking directly at me. I tip my head back, feeling my euphoria magnified by being on display.

Either Aviel doesn't notice, or he doesn't care, so I let her watch if she wants to. The sensation is raw and feels forbidden, but I only find myself getting wetter. I cry out, surrendering myself to the depths of pleasure until I can't take anymore, and I'm thrust over the edge, drenching him in my liquids. My hips buck against his lips, and his low groan vibrates through me as he drinks me in.

I grasp Aviel's hair tightly and try to jerk his head back, but he does not stop. His eyes devour me, a devilish glint of amusement hidden within the depths of those dark wells. I moan in ecstatic pleasure as he continues to lavish attention upon my core, and my head falls back on a groan. I can feel Aviel smile against me before he presses one last kiss to my core and lifts himself up. My skin tingles with anticipation as Aviel locks his smoldering gaze with mine.

"You taste like heaven." Aviel's raw voice pierces the air, deeper than I've ever heard it.

"I think I died and went there just now." I breathlessly whisper, my senses still awash in the pleasure he just gave and pulled out of me.

Aviel gives a throaty chuckle, obviously pleased by my words, and a smirk crosses his face. "Then I suppose it's good that I'm here to snatch you back." He murmurs sultrily. "We still have a ways to go, I've deprived myself of you for far too long."

In the darkness of the chamber, the air around us roils and twists, becoming suffused with power. As though sensing the shift in energy, Lilith slithers off of him and disappears into the shadows before Aviel's body shifts before my eyes – his nails lengthen into claws, and two sets of crested horns break through his hairline like blades made of onyx glass, curving back and upwards and stretching proudly towards the sky in wicked points, beckoning for me to grab hold of them.

He seems to swell with power, his tattoos taking on an eerie glow in the darkness and moving across his skin like serpents. But Aviel's eyes remain the same; piercingly dark, with a blackhole depth that seems to swallow all light around, yet the love for me in his gaze never falters, and I realize why I love this complicated creature. I know that this demonic being is still my Aviel.

"You belong to me now," he says, dragging his fingertips down the vulnerable column of my throat, the pointed tips of his claws grazing my flesh. "I'll show you what it is to be mine. Tell me you're ready for me." Something about his voice makes it impossible to think.

"Yes," I whisper, barely getting the word out as a shiver races through me.

"How shall I take you then?" he purrs, a wicked smile curling up the corners of his mouth and his fangs glinting in the half-light. His hand dips lower, and he cups one of my aching breasts and rolls my nipple between two of his fingers. I bite my lip.

"Shall I pound into you until you scream for mercy?" He hisses—his other hand descending onto my opposite breast, roughly massaging it, making me writhe beneath him in pleasure—"Or shall I fuck you slow until you go mad with pleasure?" He gives a small snort. "Or perhaps both."

"Please," I gasp, so distracted by everything that I barely register what he is saying. "I don't care—take me however you want..."

A growl rises from his throat. Drawing a claw back, he rests it where the pulse of my beating heart pounds out of control, and his snarl turns into a smile.

He curls his fingers around my waist, flipping me onto my stomach with surprising grace, and takes his place, kneeling between my legs.

I press back against him, wanting him so badly. My body quivers, breaths deepening as Aviel grips and spreads the globes of my buttocks. He thumbs the delicate flesh of them, his claws digging into me—and I know it will leave a mark. I gasp as his tongue darts out, licking and sucking along my inner folds from the back. My body feels like it's on fire, and a million shivers course through my veins. Aviel pulls me closer, the sensation of his mouth consuming me, and his tongue delving deep inside is overwhelming.

The commingling of his sinewy tongue, his fangs grazing my flesh, and his hot breath against my skin ignite an insatiable appetite within me. My toes curl, and I can feel the edges of orgasm creeping closer. I can't help but moan and writhe, winding my hips and shifting myself back against his face as he continues.

"Easy," he rumbles, and with one last lave of his tongue, he pulls away, leaving me wanting and mewling in protest.

Aviel roughly pins me down into the mattress, my cheek flush against the soft sheets, while pressing his body against my backside, forcing me to arch into his firmness. Leisurely, he lets his hand trail agonizingly slow down my back, grazing their sharpened tips along my spine as he drags his tongue along my flesh, making my arch deepen. I can't suppress the trembling that races through me, each nerve ending lit up with pleasure, and just as I try to grind back onto him, he shifts our positions again.

Seizing my wrists in a tight grip, he presses them into the small of my back and leans over me to whisper into the hollow of my neck: "Let me see how much of me you can take."

Shifting himself between my legs with a knee nudging them apart, he presses his erection against my slick opening slowly to burn a trail along my fevered flesh.

"Do you want this, Adora?" he asks, and that deep timbre of his voice makes me melt while he digs his claws deeper into my skin, holding me in place.

My body trembles; I want him so badly. I need him to fuck me hard and bury himself deep inside. I try to move, to writhe against him, but he doesn't let up. My face flushing with heat, I can only whimper.

"Mmmm . . ." I'm practically panting as I open my eyes to look back at him, my mouth thirsting for his lips, my core so empty without him.

"Do you?" He drinks in my reaction without granting me any kind of reprieve, his eyes locked onto mine—dark, burning with hunger.

"Y-Yes-"

He begins to press his tip into me, his cock swollen and engorged. Slowly he forces himself inside, inch by turgid inch, filling me more than I thought possible, and I let out a slow, guttural moan of pleasure.

But he doesn't move.

"You're so fucking wet, Adora," he bites out through gritted teeth. "So warm."

Again, he doesn't move.

I'm squirming; I can't help it. I want him to buck his hips into me, drive me over the edge, and make me forget that there was anything in this world before he was inside me.

But he stills my movements.

"Beg for more," he whispers finally.

My lips part, and I release a low, soft whine in response to Aviel's demand. My eyes flutter closed, my body completely immobilized by his authoritative hold.

He grants a small thrust and slowly hisses against my ear: "I can't hear you." His wicked smile shows the tip of his fangs.

"Please," I beg, unable to take it anymore.

At my plea, Aviel finally moves inside of me with a powerful thrust, slamming his hips against mine and taking me completely by surprise as he drives himself deep into my core, and I cry out in sheer relief. He moves in and out at a languid pace, lavishing me with torturously slow strokes that leave me shuddering and arching up to meet him, groaning in bliss. He kisses along the tendons of my neck, and I whimper helplessly, writhing and squeezing around his hot length.

He moves with an addicting rhythm as he pushes me ever closer to the brink of orgasm. He increases his tempo, each thrust more intense than the last. His rhythm is faster and deeper with every stroke until I'm lost in a pleasure-filled daze as Aviel takes me brutally.

I'm moaning senselessly, incoherent in my pleasure, as he fucks me into oblivion, every stroke pushing me closer to the edge of climax. My pussy is eagerly clutching at his cock as my sensitive walls pulse around him, and I know I'm going to come hard.

Aviel releases a feral snarl in my ear before he rips himself out of me, and I let out a scream at the tension that has yet to be relieved.

He flips me onto my back, and looming over me now, he leans down and peels my lips open with his tongue, my fingers knot into his hair, my back arching up to cry out into his mouth.

But he's not done with me. Never breaking our kiss, Aviel lifts my leg to get the perfect angle, then before I can even beg, his thick and hot length thrusts into me with a force that leaves me breaking our kiss and gasping for air.

"Am I too rough?" he asks, drawing back just enough for me to answer.

But I can't. There are no words adequate to describe the pleasure that throbs through me as he slams into my slick and aching core with brutal strength. I can only scream his name as he slams agonizingly into me again.

"I couldn't stop now if I tried," he grits in an urgent tone that hints at an impending climax, bracing a hand by my head, his movements desperately passionate.

His deep, rhythmic thrusts reverberate through the entire room, shaking the bed so intensely that I feel my teeth chattering. He speeds up his thrusts and takes me to the edge of pleasured-pain again, faster and more powerful than before. He embeds himself deeper and deeper inside me with each motion, stirring a flurry of emotions within me.

"Your mine; I'll never let you go," he whispers into my ear, then he bites my earlobe. I clench my fists, throw my head back and let out a shriek as I feel a climax tear through me, and my inner walls pulse, gripping him tightly and refusing to let go.

With a surge of intensity, the sinuous glowing ink surges along his flesh and onto me, rushing over my skin like a tide of liquid fire, caressing every inch of my body. I can feel his power swimming through me, as though through copper wire, pulsing and throbbing around every limb, awakening every muscle, and coupled with the feeling of Aviel filling me, I'm left convulsing in pleasure, overcome with a feeling so intense that I felt I might burst apart, certain I will die.

He joins our lips in another searing kiss, and my nails rake down his back, my other hand gripping the coolness of one of his solid horns, as Aviel drives himself all the way into my depths with one last powerful thrust. I feel Aviel swell within me, and he roars as he follows me over the edge, his fangs sinking into my shoulder as he finds his ultimate release, his seed filling my depths, sending me over the edge again, drowning my very soul in waves of pleasure.

The tendrils of ink on our skin stir again, this time returning to its source on Aviel's body, assuming their original shapes again and settling there until he is a canvas of intricate artwork again. It leaves behind a faint warmth that stays with me long into the dizzying aftermath of exhaustion we collapse into.

My eyelids feel heavy after such an intense experience, and my lips curve up into a satisfied smile before my vision dims to darkness. We lay like that for a while, nestled in one another's embrace, savoring each other's warmth, neither of us wanting to move—until Lilith slides over Aviel's body and past my leg as she slithers her way back to her favorite spot. Her cold skin is like a shock to the system, and we both groan in frustration.

I try to drag my heavy eyelids up and get a lovely view of Aviel's tattooed pectorals above me.

"Now I want to lie in bed all day," I sigh as I settle my head onto the hard muscles of his bare chest. The profound silence is no longer unnerving; now, I actually find peace and comfort in the stillness of it.

"We have other plans. I made a reservation, and your friends are expecting us." Aviel mutters, caressing my hair as I cuddle closer.

"Let's blow them off," I murmur, not the slightest bit eager to get up and out of this bed, even if it is to see my good friends. "You said it yourself; you hate seeing all the humans shamelessly exploiting each other on this frivolous holiday."

He lets out a husky chuckle and silences me with a possessive grip on my ass, giving me a firm squeeze, the sharpness of his claws biting into me—I can't suppress the moans spilling out of my throat.

"I did. But you love it," he breathes into my ear. "So, I'll endure it for you."

I arch into him, "That's the most swoon-worthy thing you've ever said to me. It's right up there with: 'Here's a contract to prove I want you forever'."

He smirks and presses me closer. "I can’t help that I want you all to myself for all time, even though you are a silly human who loves Valentine’s Day."

The tattoo of my name on his chest cements that, and I'm going to enjoy annoying him for every Valentine’s Day as long as I live. I wouldn’t change a thing.

"Just wait till I take you to church on Easter," I taunt him, tracing the tattoos along his body with my fingers.

A deep rumble vibrates through his chest as he seizes my waist and flips me onto my back. His blazing stare devours me as he nears, now inches away from my face. The heat of his breath cascades onto my lips, setting my skin aflame. "Only if I can take you to visit my family on Christmas."

The thought sends a tremor through me; Aviel is the only demon I can handle right now. But a new idea does come to mind.

"How about we stick to the one holiday that we both enjoy?" I reply, then look up suggestively.

"Deal," Aviel's fathomless gaze ignites a fire within me as he accepts the invitation.

My heart thrums in my chest as I bow my head to take him in. With a crooked smile, Aviel drags his fingers to the nape of my neck, gearing up to demonstrate how deeply Valentine's Day has grown on him.

Which is an impressive ten inches give or take.

Happy Valentine's Day to me, indeed.

About Author

♥

Lexis Esme is a writer of steamy erotic romance stories featuring beautiful black heroines of every variety and the gorgeous men (and supernatural beings) who love them. Lexis believes that everyone should be able to see themselves wined, dined, seduced, romanced, and even ravaged in their choice of romantic literature and love interests of every variety to cherish them. Seeing a lack of the kind of main love interests that look like her, she set out to create as many of these stories as she possibly can for readers who might feel the way she does or simply just want to see something new. Variety is the spice of life, after all, and Lexis loves to keep it spicy.

Based in Canada, she spends her days walking the nearby nature trails dreaming up romantic and sexy new adventures and scenarios, the steamier, the better. She also loves experimenting in the kitchen, dancing, drawing, and reading. She never ever has enough books, shoes, or chocolate.

She is currently hard at work on a new series of sexy novellas and various other erotic short stories.

Follow Lexi Esme on her socials and get updates on upcoming projects and more!

Linktree: https://linktr.ee/Lexiesme

Tiktok: @lexiesme

Instagram: @lexieesmebooks

Be on the lookout for Lexis's website!

THANK YOU FOR READING

♥

Thank you so much for taking the time to read this novella!

As a new writer, I'm extremely grateful that you, the reader, have even given this book a chance!

I would really, truly appreciate it if you would leave a review on Amazon, (whether you liked the book or not), it really helps me to see what my readers like and what they don't like, and I'm always striving to do better for y'all. :)

Sincerely,

Lexi Esme

Also By Lexi Esme

♥

I lean my head against the window of Gary's sleek black Mercedes and look at the passing scenery. It's a dark cloudy night, the windows are dotted with the beginnings of an autumnal shower, and my guilt is eating me alive.

"Looks like there's a storm coming," I say, breaking the silence.

"Yup," Gary says, he turns on the wipers, and they swipe at the sparse droplets on the windshield.

I hear the distant crack of thunder, and quickly say, "I don't like thunderstorms."

I shift in my seat to face him. “I'm really sorry about this, Mr. Edwards,” I begin. "I could've gotten a taxi or used a ride share app–you didn't have to go through the trouble–"

“Rhianne, really, it's fine. How were you to know that your car would break down outside in the parking lot?” he says. He raises his thick salt and pepper eyebrows and smiles at me.

“Yeah, but I feel so bad. We've been at work for almost ten hours, and now you have to take me home.”

“Eh, what's another hour of civic duty?” he says, smirking.

I sigh, and Gary pats my hand. “I'm only teasing. Really, Rhianne, it's fine. After hours, we're not just boss and employee; we're friends. Friends take care of friends. Isn't that your motto? Speaking of, I told you a hundred times to call me Gary.”

“You're right. Sorry Mr.–," I quickly correct myself with a bashful smile, "I mean, Gary,”

He laughs again, and I relax a little more into my seat.

I refocus my sights on the view outside. The city's lights slowly drown out, and all I can see are tall trees and twists of the road beyond the raindrops on the windows. The rain begins to come down with a vengeance, growing faster and more relentless with each passing second and the wipers fight desperately to keep up.

There's barely anyone else on the road, and as we continue, I notice that signage grows few and far between. I look down at my hands, folded neatly in my lap, wring them together, then give the dashboard clock another glance. It's only eight-thirty.

I shouldn't feel this anxious, and yet, I do. I lick my lips and glance at Gary.

“Uh, Gary,” I venture hesitantly, my voice just above the tinny pattering of rain against the car roof. Gary glances at me quickly in the rearview mirror, and then his eyes fall back on the road ahead.

"This isn't the way to my house." I go on, a little more sharply now. "Maybe you should turn on the GPS. I don't want you to get lost."

Gary snorts. "Relax. This is a shortcut. I take this way all the time to get to your home."

I furrow my brows, trying to think back to the last time I invited him over. I can't dredge up a memory of it.

"I'm sorry, when have you been to my house?"

His silence makes the short hairs on the back of my neck stand.

"When have you been to my house?" I repeat.

He only continues to stare forward. "Do you remember when you came to *Visionaries* to work for me?" He asks offhandedly, catching me off-guard. "I do. It was one of the best days of my life. You were so impressive during your interview. I knew I was going to hire you. And over the years, I never once regretted the decision. Not once."

I watch as the number on the speedometer increases from forty miles per hour to sixty. The click of the locks makes me jump in my seat, and I suddenly feel claustrophobic. I can't find any words to say, so I keep quiet. Gary doesn't seem to notice, because he keeps on without pause.

"It didn't take long for me to fall madly in love with you." He chuckled harshly. "And you *rejected* me."

"I don't date people I work with. It's a rule of mine...Besides, you're my boss, and I'm not comfortable with that." I wonder what happened to the traffic. I search the other lanes, but they're empty.

"Rhianne, I never once questioned your rejection until you flirted with me."

"I've never flirted with you." I try to keep my indignation— and disgust— out of my tone.

He turns and faces me. The gray of his eyes is so dark they make him look soulless. "Two years ago, April 17th, you *complimented* me on my tie. Your exact words were, 'Good pick. It goes well with your suit.' One year ago, July 24th, you called me Gary for the first time." He closes his eyes, causing the car to swerve slightly. "The way it rolled from your lips left me hard all day..."

A shiver goes down my spine. I open my mouth to say something, but I'm so flabbergasted I shut it again. Did he just say what I think he said?

"...From then on, I knew you were mine, and I always protect what is mine. I followed you home every day to make sure you were safe...and alone." His thin lips curl into a smile that makes my stomach drop. "You knew I was there. I know you did. That's why you always undress in front of the window, behind that sheer curtain. You *wanted* me to see that perfect body of yours."

His hand reaches out tremblingly before he rests it on my thigh giving it a squeeze, I jerk away from him, but he only grips tighter. "Tinkering with your car was my play in our game, but how about we skip the song and dance we've been doing for two years and get to the point? Things have gotten dicey at work, and we need to get out of town for a bit."

"I'm not going anywhere with you— " I gasp. "Don't do this. If you take me home right now, I promise all is forgiven. I won't tell anyone. We can just go back to how things were."

"But don't you get it? I want you to tell. I want you to tell the world how good I made you feel. I want you to show them you're mine." He yanks the wheel to the right, and the car careens from the road.

Slamming his foot on the brake pedal, he halts the car a mere moment before it collides into a tree. All I can hear is the sound of the rain and the beating of my own heart. In the seclusion of the woods, he unbuckles his seatbelt and faces me. Meanwhile, I pull feverishly at the door handle.

“Knock it off!” he screams, reaching for me.

I swat at his beefy hands, but he easily catches my wrist, yanking me across the seat. "Stop, Gary! Please!— " Recoiling from him, I try to twist out of his grip.

“I said fucking knock it off!” he shouts, drawing his hand back.

The sting of his slap sends my face snapping to the side, and my head rings. And for a moment, everything in me is frozen, and my brain can't form a single coherent thought. I can taste the coppery tang of blood, I feel it pooling from my nose. Tears fill my eyes, but I blink them away.

“You think you’re better than me, huh? You think I don’t deserve you? I *made* you. You are nothing without me. Maybe you need a reminder of that.”

He unlocks the door and rushes to the passenger side before I can react, and he wrenches my door open, pulling me out by my hair into the rainy night.

I try to claw my way away from him, but he throws me onto the sodden earth. My head slams against a stone, and the world around me seems to fade.

“Rhianne?”

His words are muffled, and he swims in my vision, I can barely make out his expression.

“Rhianne?!” Gary's hands fly to his mouth, and he fumbles to find my pulse. I feel myself fading, but I fight it.

"Rhi-ahhh!— "

It takes nearly all my strength, but my foot connects squarely with his groin, and I watch him crumple over.

“You bitch!” Gary rasps, holding his crotch.

I scramble to my feet, but in my disorientation, the entire world moves in a crooked circle. I stagger forward and fall on my hands and knees onto wet leaves, dirt and gravel, but I use them as leverage to push myself up to my feet once again. Thoroughly drenched and covered in dirt, I take off into the blackened woods.

"Help!" I plead as I draw further into the darkness. Leaves crunching behind me tell me Gary isn't far behind, and he laughs wildly in pursuit.

"I love this new game!"

My heart is pounding out of my chest, and my lungs burn with every breath I take, but I can't stop. My feet splashing in the puddles, I race deeper into the woods.

All at once, a flash of lightning illuminates the forest like a camera flash; the trees become stark silhouettes against a dreary sky.

"Help! Please, help!" The sound of my yelling is swallowed by the heavy rain, whipping wind, and the bone-rattling boom of thunder.

Gary's footfalls are moments away now, and I can almost feel his breath on my neck.

Please...someone...please help.

I think a silent prayer to myself, but I'm not sure to who. Just as Gary's hand grabs a fistful of my hair, I feel my feet lose purchase of the ground beneath me; it loosens and splits, crumbling beneath my feet like it's made of sand.

Before I know it, I'm tumbling down, with Gary following after.

My heart in my throat, I scream. My arms flail wildly as I try to find something to grab onto, but I slam painfully into the ground hard on my back, the air driven from my lungs. Crashing into the ground, it's every bit as painful as I imagined. I cringe and suck in my breath, my body racked with pain.

A loud bang follows, just inches from me, as Gary falls into the pit shortly after. He doesn't move.

I'm sprawled on the ground, gasping for air. To lay down, and not get up might be the kindest thing to do, but I know I'm not quite out of the woods yet.

"Gary?" I say, my voice emerges from my throat hoarse and pained.

No answer comes.

"Gary?" I try again.

Nothing.

Trying to adjust to the darkness, I blink several times, squeezing my eyes shut. I drag myself up from the ground as quickly as my aching body will allow. I strive to see in the pitch blackness of the place, but as the clouds shift overhead, a soft ray of moonlight allows me to make out a dirt-covered wall beside me.

I look down at myself. I'm covered in wet dirt, my clothes torn, and bloodied. My entire body aches from the fall, but I'm alive.

Just as quickly the clouds converge like a curtain dropping on a stage. All is in darkness again. I can't make out most of my surroundings, but it seems we've landed in a pit. It's relatively drier down here; the air hangs damply, heavily, thick with the smell of earth and nitrates.

My hands grope blindly along the walls of the place to find a steady foothold, a rock, a vine, anything. My searching fingers soon discover something hard and curved, and I smirk imagining it to be a tree root. Grabbing hold, I test some of my weight on it, but it shifts in the dirt wall, causing me to lose balance. I stagger back from it but my hand comes away sticky and with much effort.

Wonderingly, and still half dazed, I open and close my hand, feeling a clinging substance reluctantly stretching between my fingers as I pry them apart, almost like stretchy sap-covered hairs or vines. I wonder at what I just touched, I try to wipe my hand clean against my torn pencil skirt, and it very nearly adheres. I'm forced to rip my hand back, with a shuddering breath.

Something feels so wrong about this place, and I begin to wonder where I am in earnest, and as though in answer, there is a sudden and momentary flash of lightning. For a moment, I can make out the walls that surround me, and ice pours through my veins...

"Oh my God."

The pit extends far beyond, and behind me and Gary, far above us too, but what lines the pit is truly horrifying:

Shredded clothing. Bones. Disturbingly familiar-looking shapes, swathed, cocooned, in thick layers of a fine white fabric substance. And lacing the walls, miles of silvery threads.

Spiderwebs?

Recognizing the impossible material, I want to scream. Nothing comes out.

Worse still, a sound carries in the darkness just a few short feet away.

"Fuck..."

It's almost a relief to hear that it's only Gary. I can just barely make him out, struggling to sit up.

Gary groans in pain. Finally, having come to, his silhouette rises to his feet. I hear a jangling of car keys before a thin beam of yellow light cuts through the darkness. For an instant, I'm grateful Gary is here until I remember he just assaulted me and likely has plans for worse.

I back away several steps and away from the light, my hands raised to shield my eyes.

"Rhianne?...Well, at the very least, I still have you here with me...it looks like I haven't lost everything. I would have taken you with me, Rhianne, we could've lived a beautiful life together, but you don't seem to want that, which means I'll have no use for you after tonight. At the very least, this is the perfect place to leave you to rot if you continue to disrespect me."

Damn it. I guess not even circumstances can change Gary's priorities.

I retreat a fair distance from him before he redirects the beam of light elsewhere. He shines the mini flashlight along the walls, lingering on what I've just witnessed but not quite understanding what he sees. I can see it in the faint light; his hand is shaking.

“Where am-” But Gary's sentence breaks as yet another noise whispers through the darkness, a faint crackling. Following the sound with his flashlight, the beam lands at a far corner, where something shadowy quickly slips from view.

"Christ!" The flashlight drops from his hands, made clumsy in his fear. Keys and all fall to the ground in a cacophony of jingling; and all is lost to darkness once again.

"What was that?" I whisper in a harsh breath, wondering if I'd seen anything at all.

“Shit...shit!” Is all Gary says, fumbling around for his keys.

And then we both see it.

Red eyes peer back at us from the abyssal dark, and contortions of bone fill the night air.

Gary stumbles backward, and keen, rubied eyes follow his every movement.

The next part happens in slow motion, as though in a nightmare.

I watch as an enormous long pointed appendage amasses from the darkness. Black and lacquered, reflecting the faintest moonlight, it plants itself firmly in the earth.

Gary is staggering back, his heel accidentally kicking the car keys; they skitter, then bounce off into the darkness, lost.

Several uneven shafts of moonlight reveal the scene unfold before me. Gary’s eyes bulge at the sight of the other. He can’t speak. He can only watch as the creature reveals more of itself. The sight of another black leg, and then another, make his face lose all color. He turns and locks eyes with me, the fear on his face making my own double.

He opens his mouth, but no words rise from his throat. Instead, a loud gargle pierces the silence. I feel a scattered spatter of warm liquid across my face and clothing, and I damn near hyperventilate.

Shakingly, Gary looks down at his chest. Velvet blood pools and stains the ground as the creature's leg twists inside of him. It pulls Gary from his feet and brings him several feet into the air.

Blood pours from his open mouth, and he wraps his fists around the wrist-thick, serrated appendage that holds him impaled and suspended, to no avail. His grip slips off the creature like it's coated in oil.

"H-help me," he chokes out to me, twisting towards me in the creature's hold, but I can only sink to my knees, my legs having lost all feeling.

Gary is easily pulled towards the creature, toward the dark body that seems to absorb all of the light. It lashes band after band of silk webbing around him, the shiny threads glistening like silver stripes in the otherwise steady tapestry of shadows and darkness. Gary's legs kick spastically in the air, but hauntingly, the creature runs another dark appendage down Gary's horrified face in a final caress.

Its almost calm, deep growl comes back to me: "Hush, be silent now."

I watch on, horrified.

It lifts him higher, twining the fine threads in a wide sheet around and around his legs, working quickly to cocoon him compactly, like its victims in the walls. And sickeningly, I hear hollow cracking sounds, like a branch snapping in half, as the creature twists and pulls and tightens, seemingly only finding the fruitless struggles of its food amusing. The flailing Gary screams as bones are broken, but the sound is soon choked back down his throat. Gary's screams are silenced in an instant. The creature quickly wraps the last of the silky substance over his head, then continues to envelop him until he is silent. until he is still.

Gary's tightly cocooned form is hoisted on a silken rope, slung up, and secured in a high corner.

Sick to my stomach, my gaze lowers to my hand, covered in the unknown substance but now also dotted with dark blood, realizing it is the very same substance Gary is enshrouded in. I can't get the image of Gary's face, his cries, the sound of his breaking bones, out of my head.

And now the creature approaches, its slow and heavy footfalls sounding out as it turns, like it's looking to me, as though noticing me for the very first time.

In a blind panic, I turn away from the horror of the thing before me and begin to crawl on all fours. I don't see a way out, and I don't know where I am going, I just go.

Time slows.

I don't want to look up and face the creature that I know scales the walls above me. Quaking, I lift my head, my scream is amplified by the walls around me as it lunges directly at me...

To be continued...

Read the rest of this steamy romance by purchasing *THREADS OF FATE*

Made in the USA
Columbia, SC
06 June 2024